VACATIONS AND VIOLENCE

A MARGOT DURAND COZY MYSTERY

DANIELLE COLLINS

FAIRFIELD PUBLISHING

THANK YOU SO MUCH FOR BUYING MY BOOK. I AM EXCITED to share my stories with you and hope that you are just as thrilled to read them.

If you would like to know about all my new releases and have the opportunity to get free books, make sure you sign up for our Cozy Mystery Newsletter.

FairfieldPublishing.com/cozy-newsletter

CHAPTER 1

MARGOT FELT THE WARMTH OF SUNSHINE ON HER FACE AND the stiff breeze washing in over the Blue Ridge Mountains. She felt peaceful and happy. Rested in a way she hadn't been over the last few weeks while getting the bakery ready for the long weekend with her friend Celia Baxter, or CeCe as most people called her.

"There you are," CeCe called out, coming up the trail. "I thought I saw you arrive, but then you disappeared."

"It's just so peaceful up here," Margot said, grinning. "I was early and I thought you'd be busy."

"Not for you, dear friend," she said, wrapping Margot in a big hug. "I'm so glad you could make it."

"I'm happy to be here. I mean, have you *seen* this view?" she joked, knowing full well her friend got to see this view every day.

CeCe grinned and nodded. "Why do you think I took the job up here?"

"Honestly?" Margot said, turning toward her friend, "I don't know. Why did you come up here?"

CeCe looked taken aback by Margot's sharp honesty, but soon her features softened. "Oh Marg, you always could see past everything to the heart of the matter."

Margot took a seat on the log bench that gave a perfect view of the valley of blue-green mountains below them. CeCe sat down next to her, folding her hands in her lap.

"The desire for something new started when Rick and I split up."

"That was, what, two years ago now?"

"Three."

"Time certainly does go by quickly."

"And sometimes not quickly enough."

The hint of weariness in her friend's voice caused her to peer at her. Margot had first met CeCe when they took a baking class together years ago. CeCe was already a chef but had wanted to round out her career with a few extra pastry and baking classes. They'd become fast friends and had kept in touch ever since.

"But you started working here a year ago, wasn't it?" Margot asked, trying to move her friend out of the memories that possessed her.

"Yes." She nodded and looked out at the incredible view of the early morning. "Stan and Lela came up to me one night at The Vault—"

"That's where you were working as a sous chef, right?" Margot clarified.

"Yes. I was in D.C. then and working my tail off." She laughed, shaking her head. "Actually, the truth of it was that I was in charge that night. The head chef had called in sick—something he never did—and I was left in charge. And you know what? For once, I took a risk, Margot. I changed up the special and it worked; Stan and Lela loved my dish and requested to speak with the chef. Since I was the only one available, they got me."

"And that's when they offered you this position?"

She nodded, entwining her fingers in her lap. "Silly, really, to think that I could come up here and things would change."

"What do you mean? What happened?"

She bit her lip as she looked at Margot. "I didn't tell you before you came—and now I'm thinking that was a mistake—but I've been hearing things about you and all that you've done and—"

"Slow down, friend," Margot said, reaching out to place her hand over her friend's clenched fingers. "What's going on? What haven't you told me?"

"I…" She looked away and Margot thought she detected a trace of fear on CeCe's features. "Back in D.C., I was being stalked."

"You never said anything," Margot said, the shock of the news rushing at her. "Why? Why didn't you tell me? I don't live *that* far away."

"You were still in a rough spot. It was two years after Julian had died and…I didn't want to burden you."

"You can tell me anything at any time. That's what friends are for!"

"That's just it, there was nothing to tell. I mean, I wasn't sure, but I thought it was Rick. Strange notes, a shadow following me, things like that. I wasn't sure until one of the notes had a phrase he always used when talking with me. When Stan and Lela offered me the job, I jumped at it. A chance to leave D.C.? Absolutely!"

"Is that why you changed your name when you moved up here?"

She nodded. "I thought if I went back to my maiden name and stayed out of the press, I'd be safe."

"So, what's changed?" Margot said, guessing that something had happened recently by the look on her friend's face as well as her timely invitation for the weekend getaway.

"I got a n-note," she said, her voice breaking.

Margot was immediately on alert. "Was it mailed?"

CeCe shook her head. "It was…" She took a deep breath. "It was sitting on my pillow when I came back from work last week. Margot, I'm terrified. I mean, this is the best job I've ever had and I love it up here, but I'm afraid I'm going to have to disappear again."

"Do you really think it's from Rick?"

With her lips pressed together, CeCe nodded. "It's his same scratchy handwriting and addressed to—" She broke off, tears falling down her cheeks.

"Oh, CeCe," Margot said, wrapping her arm around her friend. "It's going to be all right."

CeCe shook her head. "But it's not, Margot. Can't you see? It's Rick. I just know that it's him and he's tormenting me. I-I don't know what lengths he'd go to…" She was arrested by another sob, but Margot's mind tried to fill in the blanks.

Could it really be that her abusive ex-husband had found her up here? If so, how?

"Hush now, it could be someone playing a bad prank on you," she offered, though she knew it was a weak explanation.

"But, Margot, it's Rick. It has to be. It's addressed to CeCe Bear."

Margot felt her stomach clench. She'd known CeCe back

when she'd been married to Rick and he *had* always called her that. Was it possible? Had he come up here to stalk her? And why not just have a conversation with her? Talk to her about getting back together—assuming that was his end goal.

As her mind flooded with thoughts and possible explanations, CeCe pulled back and wiped under her eyes. "I'm sorry. I should have told you all of this before, but…I wasn't sure who I could turn to and I didn't know if you'd come if…"

"CeCe," Margot said, shock lacing her words. "I will always be there for you. I hope you know that."

"I do," she said, gripping Margot's hand. "And, whether it was right or wrong, that's why I asked you up here."

Margot frowned. "What do you mean?"

"Don't you see? You're the only one who can solve the mystery of *how* Rick is doing this and how he found me."

DESPITE THE FACT that her friend had brought her to the Blue Ridge Mountain Resort under slightly false pretenses, Margot was determined to help her. She could understand CeCe's fear, but there had to be a logical explanation behind all of this and Margot was determined to figure out what that explanation was.

When CeCe had finally glanced at her watch, she'd nearly

fainted, saying she was already late for dinner prep. Promising to fill Margot in on the rest of the strange happenings that had started last week on the anniversary of her marriage to Rick, she rushed down to the lodge and left Margot to check in at the front desk.

Apparently, after CeCe had explained who Margot was to Stan and Lela, the red carpet had been rolled out for her. She was to enjoy benefits of the highest level of guest as well as full access to the grounds, various actives like horseback riding, canoeing on the lake, and even rock-climbing.

Over the time CeCe had been working at the resort, Margot had received many emails from her about how amazing Stan and Lela were to her, almost like second parents, and it seemed they felt that affection for any guest CeCe would have.

A young staff member, tall and handsome, greeted her at the check-in desk. "You must be Missus Durand," he said with an overly wide smile. "Welcome to the Blue Ridge Mountain Resort."

"Thank you," she said, surprised he recognized her. "How—"

He chuckled. "Our other guests won't be arriving until just before dinner. You're the only early check-in that I had on my list."

"Oh, I see," she said, smiling. It was fortunate for her that the resort was only a little over three hours away from

North Bank. Being a baker used to baker's hours, she'd gotten up early, which was still sleeping in for her, and made the trip before rush hour traffic could be in her way.

"I'll show you to your cabin."

He picked up her small weekend bag and led her out the double glass doors and down a mulch path. "Just a few words of caution we like to give all of our guests. Despite the luxury of our resort, we *are* out in the wilderness. We caution all guests to throw trash away in the proper receptacles and to avoid going out later at night due to the habits of more dangerous nocturnal creatures."

Margot's eyebrows rose.

"Don't worry," the young man, whose metal nametag read Chuck, said with a grin. "No one's been attacked by a bear yet."

While he laughed and turned back toward the path, Margot latched on to the word *yet*. There was a first time for everything.

"Here we are," he said, opening the door for her and holding it open so she could step inside.

The cabin was more spacious than she'd anticipated, with a vaulted ceiling in the main room that led into the tiny kitchenette at the back. A door to the right opened into the bedroom with an attached bathroom, while a set of steep stairs, almost a ladder, jutted up to the ceiling and what appeared to be a loft over the back half of the space.

"What's up there?"

"Reading nook," he said with a wink. "We have a small grocery store a few miles down the road accessible by ATV, bike, horseback, or hiking trail. Feel free to shop there and your items will be delivered within the hour. You can also feel free to take advantage of our restaurant. You are a Gold Star guest and this card--" He handed her a plastic, gold card that looked like a credit card. "--will give you access to everything without cost. Do you have any questions?"

She blinked, shocked by the opulence of a mountain retreat. She'd expected to be roughing it, but this was far from that.

"Um, not at the moment."

"Then I wish you a wonderful stay, Missus Durand." Chuck gave a slight bow and then left, closing the door behind him.

She stood in the middle of the room and admired the cabin. The large, thick logs that made up the walls looked sturdy. There were wood floors and a wooden ceiling as well, but the seemingly excessive use of wood was tempered by large, plush rugs and wall hangings that accented the cabin's rustic nature. They added a touch of elegance to the otherwise outdoorsy feel.

Then there was the view. One wall was nearly all floor to ceiling windows and looked out over the valley, miles and miles of endless trees stretching out before them. She felt as if she was the only one in this world of green.

Curiosity taking over, she climbed up the steep ladder-like stairs and grinned at what she saw at the top. A bed-like cushion stretched out against another large window. Pillows were stacked up three deep and several plush blankets sat at the end of the lounge. It was the perfect reading nook.

Giddy with excitement, she came back down the stairs only to be struck by the reality of her situation. It wasn't really a vacation if her friend was afraid for her life. But surely there had to be a good explanation for what had happened to CeCe and why this supposed stalker would be coming back now.

That was the question, though. Was Rick the one who had stalked her before? If so, was it him now as well? If it wasn't him, then who was it? And why—or *how*—had they found her here?

So many questions and not much to go on. What she needed was to see the note. That, and she had to find out more about Rick and where he'd been all this time.

Pulling her phone from her back pocket, she checked her service. None. Of course, she was high up in the mountains.

Then something flashed on her screen: Connect to BRMR.

Blue Ridge Mountain Resort. It had to be.

She selected it and was immediately taken to a login page that asked for the access code. What access code? Chuck hadn't given her—

She smiled and pulled the card from her other pocket. Sure enough, there was a code on the back. She typed it in and was rewarded by a connecting message. When it went through, she opened her email app and typed in a quick email to Detective Adam Eastwood.

She added, "Thanks again for dinner last night. I had a great time." Thoughts of their rooftop dinner at *Francine's* the night before came back to her and she smiled. He had asked her to be his official girlfriend over steaks and glasses of red wine. At the time, she'd laughed at him until she'd realized he was serious. For some reason, she'd assumed that dating one another exclusively had hinted at that reality already, but it seemed very important to him so she'd sobered quickly.

After accepting his request, he'd grinned like a child at Disneyland and she knew she'd done the right thing to accept him. Not only was Adam a first-rate detective and an upstanding member of the small community of North Bank, Virginia, but he was a kind, compassionate, and thoughtful man. She'd had no doubts about agreeing to call herself his girlfriend, though using that term in her forties seemed a bit juvenile. Then again, if she wasn't his wife and she was more than a friend, having a title did help things in that respect.

Margot turned her phone on silent and went about settling into the cabin with enough time left to grab a few hours of reading before dinner was served and she would see CeCe again. Then, Margot thought, the real search would begin.

CHAPTER 2

DINNER WAS AN EVENT IN AND OF ITSELF. THE LARGE SPACE was occupied by round tables topped with white tablecloths, sparkling silverware, and shining glasses. The sound of light chatter greeted Margot as she came through the door, glad she'd taken the time to slip into a floor length, springtime dress. It wasn't fancy, but she felt as if she fit the more formal setting. She definitely hadn't packed for this level of 'cabin vacation.'

"Missus Durand," a young woman said, coming up to her with a big smile. "My name is Alice. CeCe described you to me so I would know who you were."

"It's nice to meet you, Alice," Margot said, feeling a bit like a celebrity.

"I've heard amazing things about you and your pastries from CeCe," the girl said with a giggle. "I keep wanting to come down to your shop and try them. It's just tough to get the time off."

"I bet," Margot said, her stomach growling at the delightful smells coming from the kitchen.

"Follow me," Alice said with a sweet smile. "CeCe's set you up at a table with a few other guests so you won't be eating alone."

Margot followed the girl to one of the larger tables with a few empty seats still left. To her right was an older gentleman chatting with a younger woman on his right. Next to them was an older couple, and next to them was a young woman more focused on her phone than she was what else was going on around the table.

"Everyone," Alice said, doing a good job of sounding professional as well as formal, though she almost knocked over a glass of water when she helped Margot to sit. "This is Missus Margot Durand. She'll be joining your table for the duration of your stay. Enjoy tonight's meal."

Margot nodded at the two couples and noticed the woman still hadn't looked up from her phone. She sat and reached for her napkin just as a handsome man breezed past her and joined the table in the remaining free seat.

"What did I miss?" he asked, looking around the table.

"You're late," the woman said, her eyes still glued to the phone.

"Thanks, *honey*," he said with added emphasis. He looked at Margot. "You're new."

She was shocked, wondering how he could know that.

"We come up here almost every other weekend because it's the only retreat with Wi-Fi. I'm Matt Homes and this is my wife Sarah. She runs an online business and is rarely away from her phone. Aren't you, *sweetie*?" He flashed a tolerant smile. "I can go out and do manly things like horseback riding and archery, and she can...work." Now he grinned and rolled his eyes in a manner that said he was only joking. "I haven't met you two either," he said, directing his question to the older man and the younger woman.

"Ron Durk and my, uh, girlfriend, Jenny."

The woman seemed to cringe, or maybe Margot had imagined it, as the older man put his arm around her, but the look was gone as soon as Margot thought she'd seen it and Jenny was leaning into the man. "Yep. Jenny Blane. It's nice to meet you both."

The woman dropped her gaze to her mug of coffee, pouring an extra amount of cream in and clanking her spoon around.

"We're the Tallisons," the gentleman next to Jenny said, drawing Margot's attention. "Edgar and this is my wife Fran. This is our first time here, but so far, we're loving it."

"Speak for yourself," Fran said with a grin. "I think your favorite part was flying around those dangerous curves on the drive up here. And that would be my *least* favorite part."

Edgar grinned and wagged his eyebrows. "So what if I'm a bit of a lead-foot."

Margot held back her laugh. "Nice to meet you all. It's my first time up here as well. I'm friends with the chef, actually. And my name's Margot, as Alice said."

"Does that mean you get us free dessert?" Fran quipped.

Margot laughed. "I think it's all included."

Just then someone stood behind a podium on a slightly raised stage. It was a tall woman wearing a business suit that matched the uniform colors of the other staffers, a deep burgundy color. She was likely the coordinator.

"That's Marcy," Matt said, pouring more water for himself from the decanter in the middle of the table.

"On behalf of the Blue Ridge Mountain Resort staff, I'd like to welcome you all. It is our greatest joy to serve you while you are here. If there is anything you need, please don't hesitate to contact one of us. Before we begin, there are just a few safety rules to go over," she continued.

Having heard the information from Chuck, Margot let her mind wander to what her friend had told her before she'd rushed off to fix dinner. Margot had puzzled over it until she'd settled down with a book just to take her mind off the lack of information. But now, without something else to distract her, she found her thoughts trailing back to what CeCe had said.

She thought she was being stalked. But to what end? Had Rick contacted her wanting to get back together again? Margot hadn't been privy to all the details of their divorce but, if she remembered correctly, he had cheated on her with several women from his work. At the time, she couldn't remember if he had wanted to reconcile; she thought she remembered CeCe saying that she had considered it, but Rick wasn't interested. It made no sense then that he would come after her like this. Then again, Margot had to admit she didn't know all of the information.

That was the worst part. CeCe had dropped the idea in her lap and then run off. Granted, she had no alternative, she had to work, but it was maddening to be on the cusp of something and have it disappear for a time.

She blinked back to the present and noticed that Marcy was finishing up her introduction. "Remember, if you are interested in any of our outdoor actives, feel free to let a staff member know. We'll get you on the list and you'll be able to enjoy the full benefits of the beauty of the Blue Ridge Mountains. Thank you again for joining us and please enjoy your meal prepared by our highly decorated chef, Celia Baxter.

Marcy stepped down to a torrent of applause and the light dinner conversation returned. Margot focused on enjoying the meal and getting to know those at her table, though conversation was stilted at best. Perhaps things would improve in the morning after a relaxing evening.

"WHAT DID YOU THINK OF DINNER?" CeCe said, coming up to Margot from the kitchen, her white chef's coat unbuttoned at the collar.

"It was wonderful—fabulous—you truly are a master."

CeCe blushed with pride and Margot could almost imagine that things were back to normal, but she couldn't forget what her friend had said. She was being stalked and the culprit had followed her to the resort.

During the silence through most of the dinner Margot had thought through questions she needed answers to, but looking at her friend now, it was obvious to see that she needed a night of rest before Margot gave her the third degree. Margot almost smiled at that thought, knowing it was a saying Adam often used in jest.

"Before we go," CeCe said, interrupting Margot's thoughts, "could I introduce you to someone? Well, two someones actually?"

"Of course," Margot said, looking around the quickly emptying dining room to see if she could spot who CeCe would introduce her to.

"They aren't here," she explained. "Follow me."

They walked out of the double, wooden doors that closed off the dining hall and entered the lodge's main sitting area. A large river stone fireplace dominated one wall adjacent to another wall made completely of windows. It looked out onto a view similar to the one from Margot's cabin. An impressive valley below, filled with green trees, was now covered mostly in shadow due to the setting sun.

Large, comfortable couches and chairs took up most of the area, providing seating for many to relax and enjoy a book or a specialty coffee from the café that was still open as some of the guests milled about.

"They have an apartment upstairs," CeCe explained.

Margot frowned and wanted to ask who, but she was cut off by CeCe looking around like they were breaking some rule and motioning Margot under the rope.

"Uh, should I be going up here?" Margot eyed the sign attached to the rustic looking rope that said, "Employees Only."

"You're with me. You're fine," CeCe said with a grin.

Margot followed her friend up the carpeted stairs that wound behind the fireplace, the stones wrapping all the way around the back. When they got to the top, there was a door to the right. It wasn't marked in any way, but CeCe paused, grinned at Margot, and knocked.

A few moments later, the door opened and CeCe's grin widened.

"CeCe *darling*," a woman said as aged hands came into view. "I'm so glad you came to visit."

"I brought a friend I'd like to introduce you to."

At this, a woman's head popped out into the doorframe, a smile already in place. "You must be Margot!"

With one swift movement, CeCe propelled Margot into the room. She took in the large space that she assumed occupied the whole top half of the dining hall. A fireplace dominated most of the far back wall, likely occupying the chimney space of the fireplace in the dining hall. Then, elegant couches and chairs took up residence in the center. To each side there were doors leading to what Margot assumed were bedrooms. There was no kitchen, but she assumed they hardly needed that with the dining hall's kitchen below.

"Welcome to our little home."

Margot nearly laughed at this, thinking the space had to be over four thousand feet, but she merely nodded. "It's lovely to be here. You are?" She looked accusingly at CeCe for an explanation.

"Oh, sorry," CeCe laughed. "This is Lela Wilkinson. Where's Stan?"

"He'll be right out, I'm sure. He was in his study, but I told him there was someone at the door."

"Is that my CeCe girl?" a booming voice said behind them.

They turned to see a tall man with white-gray hair wearing a dark green cardigan over a bright pink plaid shirt. He exuded style, Margot thought with a smile.

"Stan, this is my dear friend Margot Durand."

"I hear you make the best pastries this side of France. I may need a demonstration to truly believe this."

Lela leaned against Stan, her salt and pepper hair pulled back in an elegant bun and her clothes just as stylish as Stan's. "My husband likes his pastries, Margot," she said with a laugh. "Despite what his doctor says about eating them."

"Everything in moderation, right CeCe?"

Margot looked over to her friend and saw CeCe nodding, the unmistakable look of caring on her face. *She really loves Stan and Lela,* Margot thought.

"We're so glad you get to come and visit with our dear CeCe," Lela said. "She barely gets down to town and I fear she'll get lonely."

"Oh, I'm fine." CeCe's smile was forced and Margot wondered if Lela and Stan could see that too.

"Well, I just wanted to introduce her. We're going to head back to our cabins, but I hope we can have a meal or coffee or something together."

"You betcha," Stan said without hesitation. "Throw in some pastries and I'm liable to hire you."

Margot laughed. "I have my own bakery to run, but I appreciate the enticement. Why don't I make some pastries for you regardless?"

"Done!" Stan let out a hearty laugh and they made their exit.

When they were outside, CeCe looped her hand through Margot's arm and grinned at her. "Aren't they the best? I feel like they've all but adopted me since offering me this job!"

"They seem really wonderful. I bet you feel that..." She hesitated, wondering if she would be bringing up bitter memories.

"That they are a sort of replacements for *my* parents?" she asked, looking up at Margot.

"I wasn't going to say it quite like that."

CeCe laughed. "No, it's all right. I've felt that about them, actually. Not a replacement so much as a second chance at having parents again. It's not a replacement, but...it helps."

"I'm glad you've found—" Margot trailed off, her attention snagging on something in the bushes to the right of the path. They were almost to their cabins and she'd done a cursory glance around them out of habit. "What is that?"

"I-I don't know." CeCe slipped her arm free of Margot's and walked toward the item on the path. It was a deep burgundy color.

"CeCe," Margot warned, putting out a hand toward her friend. "Don't—"

Her friend's scream shattered the night and Margot rushed into the bushes after her, stopping short when she saw what her friend had.

A man lying face down on the ground.

CHAPTER 3

"Now you say you just *happened* to see him there?"

Margot's head snapped up at the man's tone. Detective Sal Rexton of the Gold Springs Police Department stood with his arms akimbo, staring down at CeCe like *she'd* been the one to blame for the man's body lying in the woods.

"No, Detective," Margot said, coming to stand next to her friend and wrapping her arms around her shoulders. "Don't treat CeCe like *she's* the killer here."

"The *killer,* you said?" He pulled down his wire-rimmed glasses and pierced her with a blue-eyed stare. "What makes you say anything about killing?"

Margot frowned. Surely he was joking. But the longer she looked back at him, waiting for him to claim he'd been joking, he didn't move—he barely blinked.

"Well, I thought it was obvious." Licking dry lips, she

turned to look back at where they'd found the body. Lab techs had set up bright lights to shine down so that they could accurately process the scene, though she did notice a striking lack of caution. "Surely you noticed the blunt force trauma on his forehead there." She pointed a finger in the direction of the man's temple. "And the fact that, on his right hand, his knuckles are bruised as if they connected with something hard—recently. Clearly he took a punch at whoever came against him."

"*Clearly* my boot," Sal said. "What you think you're seeing is wrong, Miss Margot. He fell, hit his head on this here tree--" He indicated a place where blood had been wiped against the tree. "--and fell here to succumb to his death. We'll know more once the M.E. takes a look, but don't let that pretty little head of yours get in a twist creating murders where there are none."

The cadence of his speech reminded Margot of old southern gentlemen who had little regard for a woman being anywhere but the kitchen. Granted, Margot did spend quite a bit of time in the kitchen, but it was for her business—not the happiness of a man. She licked her lips, almost smirking at her feminist thoughts. *Calm down, he's just seeing what he wants to see.*

"I'll defer to your judgment," she said in a placating tone.

Her merely humphed and turned back to CeCe. "And what were you two doing out here so late?"

Margot frowned and pressed her lips together. No need to antagonize the man.

"W-we weren't out that late. I mean…" CeCe swallowed and her gaze swept to the man on the ground before fleeing back to the detectives. "We were coming back from dinner. I suppose we stayed a little later talking with Lela and Stan. I wanted to introduce them to Margot."

"And why is that?" Detective Sal was leaning forward, his eyes nearly slits as they dug into CeCe's. Margot fought the urge to come to her friend's defense. As if she *or* CeCe needed defense. She knew they would find that the man had been dead for at least two hours before, judging on what she could see from his injuries. They all had alibis during that time. The question was, who *didn't?*

"Because she's my friend. Is there a reason you're questioning *me* like this, Detective Rexton?"

"No." He straightened and flipped to a new page in his small notebook. "Now, Miss Margot," he said, forced southern charm dripping from his words, "why exactly are you here at the resort?"

She was about to open her mouth to answer when another thought struck her. Her gaze flickered to CeCe's then back to the detective. Should they tell him about CeCe's stalker? Or was that unrelated? Margot knew that all information was helpful in such cases, but she wasn't sure that CeCe was even legitimately being stalked. She hadn't yet seen any evidence and if CeCe hadn't felt the need to share, should she?

It felt slightly dishonest, but she wanted to double-check what her friend was experiencing before muddying the waters. At the moment, Sal thought that this was an accident—and there was always the chance that Margot was wrong. She never wanted to be too proud to admit something like that.

"I'm here to visit my dear friend CeCe," she said with a forced smile to match the detective's. It was clear he didn't like her.

He grunted and jotted down a note.

"Do you know the deceased?" he asked, looking back at CeCe.

Margot's friend nodded, swallowing and trying to keep her gaze from traveling back to the dead man. "Y-yes, his name is Darren. He's a relatively new hire who came on last season and they hired him back for this year. He is— was—a really great guy." CeCe gave in to the tears that had pooled in her eyes and Margot took up her place next to her friend again.

"We've already given our statements. Is there anything else you need us to tell you?" Margot asked, gesturing toward her friend. "I think we need to go rest."

He looked at the scene where his techs were still at work and then down the road to the row of onlookers. Stan and

Lela were making their way down the path at that moment as well.

"No. I'll have a conversation with the owners and, should I need to, I'll be in touch."

"Thank you," Margot said, to which he replied with a grunt and went off to meet with the Wilkinsons.

"Can we go?" CeCe asked, her shoulders shaking.

"Yes, let's get you to your cabin."

Margot maneuvered her friend in the direction of her cabin, but took a moment to scan the crowd. It looked like the usual collection of curious faces. She recognized some of them from their dinner earlier and a few new faces that she either hadn't seen in the dining hall or who had arrived later.

She did spot Jenny Blane, and Fran and Edgar Tallison standing off to the side, but no one else from her table. Pulling her attention away, she helped CeCe open her door when her hands shook too much, and directed her inside.

"Why don't you sit down and I'll make you some chamomile tea. It'll help settle your nerves."

"All right. I'm going to change first," CeCe said, the weariness in her voice evident. She disappeared into her room and Margot searched the cabinets for her friend's favorite tea.

A muffled scream came from the bedroom the next moment. Margot dropped the box of tea and ran toward the door to find CeCe in a heap on the floor.

~

"CeCe!" Margot rushed to her side, grabbing her shoulders and shaking gently. "What's wrong? Are you hurt?"

As if coming out of a faint, CeCe blinked and lifted her hand to cover her face. "I— Oh, Margot!"

"What is it? What happened?"

Tears began to fall down her friend's cheeks and she sniffed, a shaking finger pointing to the bed.

There, nestled on the pillows atop the made-up bed, was a white teddy bear. A flicker of a memory made Margot frown. "Isn't that—"

"Yes," CeCe sobbed. She heaved in a breath and looked up at Margot. "He's found me. Margot, Rick's found me!"

Margot looked from her friend to the teddy bear. "Hold on now," she said, reaching for the bear. She knew that fingerprints wouldn't be visible on the bear, though when she picked it up, she did notice a card. Careful not to touch more than the edges, she opened the small card.

Miss me?

MARGOT SWALLOWED HARD. It wasn't exactly a threatening note, and yet it was. It obviously hinted at the fact that there was a prior relationship—or marriage, in this case—but it wasn't signed, and anyone could have put it there.

"CeCe, are you sure that—"

"It's his handwriting," she said, her hand gripping a cross necklace at her throat. "I'd know it anywhere."

Margot went to the closet and put the bear on the top shelf. She didn't know why, but throwing it away seemed unwise. And still, if there was something in it or on it, keeping it there shouldn't hurt.

"What are you doing?"

"I'm making you that cup of tea and you are going to tell me *everything* that's happened since you first found out Rick was stalking you."

"You mean when it first started?"

"Yes."

"Okay." She took a deep breath and reached for the pile of clothes she'd already pulled out of a drawer before she saw the bear, Margot assumed.

Nodding once, Margot went back to the kitchenette area and made both of them steaming cups of tea with honey and lemon, then joined her friend in the living room area where each took up a side of the cushioned leather couch.

"I'm sorry, Margot," CeCe started.

"Don't be." Margot smiled back at her friend. "I'm honored you'd think of me to come and help you during this time. I'm sure there's an explanation for all of this."

"But if he's able to get in my room?"

"Right…" Margot nodded. "I've been thinking about that, actually, and I think you should come and stay with me. Since I'm here with you, I think we're fine, but once we're done talking, you can come and stay in the super comfy loft. Will that work?"

CeCe nodded. "That would make me feel a lot better."

"So…" Margot pushed past the silence. "Tell me what happened."

CeCe looked down at the mug in her hands and frowned. "We'd been married five years when I realized something was wrong," she began. "He would be gone really late and sometimes have to go into the office on the weekends. I didn't think anything of it at first, he was part of a startup and that's what happens. But then I called one night and he wasn't there. In fact, I asked about him working the previous weekend and no one knew about it. It was bizarre. Then I started to put two and two together."

"He was having an affair," Margot filled in.

"Yes." She sniffed and Margot saw the tears in her eyes. "I wanted to work it out, to move past it, you know? But he was done. When the divorce was final, I continued to pursue my career and tried to move on."

Margot felt for her friend, the devastation of losing her own husband to death had been tragic and painful, but she hadn't wondered at his fidelity.

"But then a year later, I started getting the notes. Just one here and there—on my car windshield, in my mailbox, you know. I knew immediately it was Rick. He talked about what he'd lost and how sorry he was, but he never came right out and said what he wanted. It was maddening and I had no way to make him stop because I didn't know where he was or how to get in touch with him. They escalated to where he sent me a bouquet of black roses and that's when I knew I needed to do something—if only for my own sanity. I took all the evidence, notes and everything, and gave them to the police. I got a restraining order, but that wouldn't really help. That's when I met Stan and Lela and the rest you know."

Margot took a moment to mull over her friend's words. "Did he continue to bother you once you went to the police?"

CeCe thought back, her eyes searching the distance. "Yes. He sent a few more notes and 'gifts.' Stupid things—something like that teddy in there--" She shivered. "--but when I accepted the position here, I waited until two in

33

the morning and left. All of my stuff—everything—was left behind. I eventually had movers pack it up and put it in a storage facility. I've only been back there once to get a few things, and made sure no one followed me. I even made up a name to put it under. Margot, it's like I'm living in some type of television show. How did he find me? I've been so careful."

Margot nodded, puzzling through what her friend had shared. "And, from what you know, Stan and Lela haven't posted your photo or your real name anywhere? Not on the website or in any magazines or something?"

CeCe shook her head. "I've been very clear with them that I must remain anonymous. They like it, actually. They say it adds mystery. I'm very careful around the guests as well. As far as I know, my real self is a ghost."

"Taxes?"

"Filed through a CPA with a P.O. Box in a town about an hour away. He understands the situation."

Margot nodded again. From all angles, it would seem her friend really had disappeared as best she could. But there were still ways to find a person—she knew that firsthand from the last case she'd helped on where her assistant, Dexter Ross, had found two people from an incident forty years before.

"All right," Margot said, shaking her head. "I'll have to think this through. In the meantime, let's go to my cabin and get some rest, all right?"

CeCe nodded, but gripped Margot's hand before they could stand. "Marg, I hope I haven't put you in any danger."

Margot smiled. "I don't think you have, but if so, it wouldn't be the first time I've been in a dangerous situation and it certainly won't be the last."

CHAPTER 4

MARGOT WOKE TO SUNLIGHT STEAMING THROUGH THE
windows overlooking the valley. It was a beautiful, serene
setting but the view was marred by Margot's thoughts of
the events from the night before. Clearly Detective Sal
Rexton thought that the staff member's death had been
accidental. His questions had all been in line with that,
despite the evidence she'd pointed out.

Then there was CeCe's explanation with what had
happened with her ex-husband. Had he truly wanted to
get back with her, wouldn't he have eventually made
contact? Or was his purpose for the notes and gifts merely
to torment her? But why?

And, despite all of those things, the questions that
remained were of equal value. Was it Rick bothering
CeCe now? If so, how had he found her? And was this
crude stalking of her linked to the staff member's death or
were they two separate crimes?

Margot wasn't one to place the blame for things on coincidences, and yet sometimes, they did happen.

She leaned over and picked up her phone, the fluffy comforter sending out a whoosh of air as she leaned down to read through her messages. Since she had closed up her shop for the weekend, she hadn't expected much.

There was an email about a delayed order, a few requests for special pastries for parties, and then an email from her staff member. Tapping the screen, she brought up Rosie's email. It was a short message telling her to relax, have a good time, and not to worry about anything—including Bentley. Margot laughed. The older, African American woman had been a staple at the shop for years now, taking on shifts most afternoons so Margot could have a break. She was also friends with one of their regular customers, Bentley Anderson.

Margot pictured the older, retired lawyer, his gray hair always mussed and his nose stuck in a crossword puzzle. She wondered how he was faring for a whole weekend without his usual order of coffee and a caramel pecan pastry. It was funny how just the thought of pastries set her fingers to itching. She wanted to bake—always did in the mornings—but this was her vacation, or so she told herself.

She typed back a quick response to Rosie then double-checked to see if Adam had gotten back to her. There was still no reply and she went as far as opening a new window to send him another email when she heard the creaky ladder stairs that indicated CeCe was awake. Adam would get to her email when he could—or it was possible he still didn't have any information to convey—and she needed to have patience.

Closing her email app, she pulled on a sweater to ward off the morning's chill and went to meet her friend.

"Morning," she said, noting the bags under CeCe's eyes. "Did you sleep well?"

CeCe shrugged. "Not particularly, but it wasn't due to lack of trying. That mattress up there is extremely comfortable, but I just kept seeing images of Darren and…" She pressed a hand to the base of her throat. "I barely knew him, but seeing something like that sticks with you."

"It does," Margot said, coming up to her friend and wrapping an arm around her. "We'll get to the bottom of this, I promise."

"But, Margot…" CeCe pulled away to look up at her friend. "Do you think Darren's death had something to do with Rick stalking me?"

Margot forced a smile. "I have no idea. It may have been an accident like Detective Rexton said…" She almost added, *or not*, but thought better of it, knowing her friend's worried state already. "But the main thing is to find out *how* that teddy bear got into your room. Who has access to the rooms?"

CeCe frowned. "Housekeeping of course, but I happen to know they are very careful about room keys. It's not easy to get into someone's cabin."

"Do you have to cook for breakfast?"

CeCe looked at the clock on the microwave and nodded. "I should be leaving soon."

"Okay, you go and I'll stop by your cabin on my way there."

"But why?"

"To see if any of the doors or windows were forced. If not, we'll know to talk to housekeeping."

"All right, but be safe."

Margot smiled. "I always am."

Her friend showered and changed while Margot got ready for the day and then the two walked down the path. They split off and Margot went to CeCe's cabin while her friend went on to the dining hall. Margot had offered to go with her, but CeCe declined, saying that she would be fine. Seeing a few staff members out, Margot felt inclined to agree.

Margot walked back down the path toward CeCe's cabin and took it in from the perspective of someone who would want to break in. It wouldn't be difficult, seeing as how the cabin was encased by several larger trees. Margot's cabin was similar, though the back of hers faced the incredible valley view where as CeCe's backed up to the woods.

Being careful to take note of her surroundings in case she was observed, Margot began to systematically check the doors and locks. There was the front door, but it was accessed by the same type of swipe card Margot had. Those locks were much harder to break in to and, if tampered, she was sure there would be visible evidence. She saw nothing.

Making her way around to the side window facing the front, she noticed that everything seemed to be in order. She even tested it but it didn't budge, the seal unbroken. She walked around counter-clockwise, noting the large set of glass windows that could not be opened. They looked in order as well. When she reached the back, she noticed that there was the same type of lock as the front door. This door led to a small, screened-in porch, though the door to the porch was the crude type without a lock. All windows there and on the other sides of the cabin were untouched.

Sighing, she placed her fists on her hips and looked around. The woods behind the cabin were dense and foliage had grown thickly in most places. It didn't look easy to approach through, but maybe...

On a whim, she made her way to the tree line and walked the perimeter where the grass was mowed from one end to the other. At the far side, she saw what she was looking for. A concealed path. It was small and little used, but it *was* a path. She thought that whoever had made it would assume someone would take it for a deer trail, but Margot noted a few broken branches in a wider path than a deer's hoof would make, and even the print of a boot heel.

It was nothing conclusive, but it was something.

MARGOT WALKED around the corner of CeCe's cabin and ran into someone who let out a grunt and a rush of air even as her hands flew up to block the attacker. Her Krav Maga classes had instilled a fast response time for situations like this and she was prepared to defend herself when her eyes registered that she knew the person in front of her.

"Mister Homes?"

Matt Homes stared back at her, his eyes flicking down to her hands raised in a defensive pose. "Uh, should I be worried?" he said with a forced laughed.

She relaxed her stance, though the underlying tension remained. What was he doing here so close to CeCe's cabin?

"I thought you and Sarah were on the other side of the complex?" she said, bluffing.

"We are," he said, looking confused that she would know that, "but I was out for a walk."

She tried to pick up on any deception beneath the words, but she couldn't tell if he was telling the truth or not. "Probably should head back to the cabin to change for breakfast, though." He forced an uneasy smile, indicating his sweaty workout clothes, and took a step back.

Margot merely watched him, finding that sometimes silence brought out more information than words, but he didn't say anything else, just turned and hustled away toward the other side of the resort complex.

Odd.

She glanced back at the nearly hidden trail she'd uncovered, then at the cabin again. She knew where she needed to go next.

The front desk staff looked bright and cheery despite the early hour of the morning.

"Hello, Missus. Durand," Chuck said, his wide grin overly bright. "How can I help you?"

She flashed a smile of her own and leaned against the counter made of smoothed burl wood. It was impressive and added a rustic touch to the space. Now that she'd met Lela Wilkinson, she wondered if she had picked it out. The woman seemed to have excellent taste.

"I was wondering if you could help me with a strange question."

Chuck leaned forward, peering around as if checking that

no one was within earshot of their conversation. "You can expect my greatest confidence."

"I'm sure." She smiled and picked up her room key. "Who has access to my room?"

His expression clouded immediately. "Why? Was something wrong? Something missing?"

"Missing? No, but have other guests reported thefts?"

He looked as if he regretted saying anything. "I'm afraid I'm not at liberty to say."

"Chuck…" Margot leaned forward and looked him in the eye. "I'm merely asking out of curiosity. If I wanted to get into someone else's cabin, there wouldn't be a way, would there?"

He cringed again, but she widened her smile and he seemed to consent. "I mean, you are a friend of CeCe's so…no. It's not easy. We've ensured the safety of our guests—many who pay quite a bit to vacation here—by ensuring that both of their doors, front and back, are ensured with a key-coded, tamper-proof lock. The only people with access are our cleaning staff, who are expertly vetted, mind you."

"Surely *you* or someone at the check-in desk has access?"

"Not necessarily." He looked around again before refocusing on her. "Any key we've made is registered in our system. It's impossible to make one without it being entered into the system. And further--" He leaned even closer. "--we have a log that shows when the keys are used."

"An electronic log?"

He nodded. "It's really for our patrons' safety as much as it is for our staff standards. Each member of our staff has an access card that can be 'loaded' with access so it can be tracked."

Margot frowned. "Can you explain that?"

"Sure," he said, shrugging. "I could load access to your room onto my staff card. I already have main door access as well as a few other locations for my job, but I could have your cabin coded onto my card. Not that I would," he added quickly, heat rising up his cheeks.

She ignored the blush. "And if you accessed my cabin, it would show up?"

He nodded. "Yes. We don't often need to do this, but we can condense our access points per staff member, cabin, area, or whatever criteria. It's actually helped to greatly reduce laziness in our staff, knowing we can check when they swipe into a cabin for cleaning, as well as theft…" he trailed off and cringed.

"Have things gone missing then?"

He shrugged. "Some guests have mentioned a few things, but it seems impossible. There's no irregular entries to be found."

Margot thought through what he'd said, but couldn't see a way around the reality that somehow someone *was* gaining access to CeCe's cabin. She wanted to ask Chuck for a readout to her friend's cabin, but had a feeling that wouldn't be possible—at least not yet.

"Seems like a complex system," she mused.

"Oh it is!" he said eagerly, as if happy she wasn't pushing the theft aspect of the conversation. "In fact, it was created by—"

"There you are, Margot!" CeCe came into the foyer area, smiling. "I've saved you a seat for breakfast and I'm going to join you."

Margot looked back at Chuck and gave him a grateful grin before following her friend into the already crowded dining hall. It might be time for breakfast, but the last thing on her mind was how fluffy the eggs were. No, she was much more concerned with the reality that someone was gaining access to CeCe's cabin—as well as others—without leaving a trail.

One thing she knew for certain—it wasn't a ghost. Now to prove that.

CHAPTER 5

Breakfast had filled her up so much that, when asked about sitting and reading in the lodge with CeCe for a little while during her break, Margot regretfully refrained.

"I *have* to walk off this breakfast or I won't be hungry for lunch," she'd quipped. CeCe, still looking tired from her restless night of sleep, waved her on with a warning to stay on the paths.

Margot didn't need to be told twice. As she slipped off her light sweater, enjoying the warmth from the vigorous walk on the bark path that led around the entire complex, her mind began to wander.

There was absolutely no way anyone could get into CeCe's room without an access card. All entries would be logged in the computer if it were someone with a card. She knew that her next move had to be getting a look into the computer, but she had a feeling that wasn't going to be easy. She'd either have to resort to some very sneaky measures to get Chuck away from the front desk and hope that she could find her way around the program *or* she could ask CeCe to talk to Lela and Stan.

Margot had a feeling that, where CeCe was concerned, they would completely understand and want to look into her cabin's access. In fact, if Margot had read them correctly, she had a feeling they would want nothing more than to protect CeCe to the fullest extent.

Was that why CeCe hadn't said anything to them yet? Why she'd insisted Margot come up to the resort on the hopes that she could figure out who was tormenting her friend? But didn't CeCe realize that it would likely be a case for the police if it *were* Rick? And if it wasn't...

That thought caused Margot to stop. If it wasn't Rick, who was it? She realized that she'd been so focused on CeCe's insistence that it was her ex-husband come back to, in essence, haunt her, she hadn't allowed her mind to think outside of that box. She knew better than that.

Margot continued her walk, her mind flitting around possibilities. Was someone here at the camp interested in scaring CeCe away? Margot made a mental note to talk to those in the kitchen. Was it possible that someone was vying for her job? CeCe hadn't mentioned anyone, but it was possible she didn't know.

Or, was it possible someone was truly stalking her—

possibly a male coworker that CeCe didn't realize was interested in her? He could see his little gifts as a means to connect with her. Then again, that seemed unlikely as well considering the similar nature of the gifts to what Rick had given CeCe. That was something that truly bothered Margot. It was the biggest connection to Rick and made it almost impossible to see any other alternative.

As Margot turned the corner of a building, she nearly ran headlong into Ron Durk and Jenny Blane.

"Watch it," Ron said, then, "oh, it's you Margot. What are you doing back here?"

She wanted to say she could ask him the same thing, but they both looked startled. "I was just out on a walk. Trying to work off some of those heavy calories from breakfast."

"Didn't you say you're a baker?" Jenny said. "I mean, I'd think you were used to eating a lot." She forced a smile but it didn't reach her eyes.

"I learned a long time ago to *sample* my treats, not to eat them every day."

Though she did remember a time in college when she gained almost twenty pounds while they were learning to make her favorite dessert, *crème brûlée*. It had taken a lot of hard work, some very encouraging friends, and a mentor who had been down the same path to help her see a healthier approach to being a baker.

"Oh," Jenny said, crossing her arms over her chest.

"What are you two doing out here?" she asked, her tone bright.

"Just talking a walk," Ron said, shifting weight on his feet and scratching the side of his nose. "We're going horseback riding later," he blurted.

"Oh, sounds exciting," she said, looking between them and again trying to decipher their relationship. "I suppose I'd better keep going—got to keep the heart rate up and all."

"Sure, sure," Ron said, waving her on. Jenny merely watched her go without a word.

Odd.

Margot tried to yank her thoughts back to the present, but she just couldn't. Instead, she pulled out her phone and checked for messages. It was odd to be out in the middle of nature like this and yet still have internet access. It wasn't perfect coverage, but enough to send and receive emails.

As she opened the app, she was pleased to see a reply waiting for her from Adam. Rather than risk walking and reading at the same time, she put the phone away and fast-walked the rest of the way back to the lobby.

Breathing hard but excited to see what he'd said, she ordered an iced coffee and sat in an overstuffed leather chair at the back of the lodge.

Once the waiter had brought her coffee out, she took a long sip and then brought up Adam's email.

HEY MARGIE,

Great to hear from you, though I'm already worried about what you sent me. First off, you're supposed to be having a relaxing weekend! But, I'll save the lecture for another email.

Secondly, I ran the name you sent me and I find the results odd, if not a bit distressing. Rick Moody disappeared about 2 weeks ago.

MARGOT LOOKED up from the email, her eyes wide. That would slightly coincide with when CeCe's stalker had reappeared.

I PHONED his last place of employment as well as his former landlord. Both said he up and left without a word. No warning and nothing removed from his apartment, as far as the landlord could tell.

So, here's the part where I warn you not to stick your nose into risky business—and here's the same part where you ignore me.

DON'T IGNORE ME, MARGIE!

But I know you will, so please be careful and contact me the soonest chance you get. I want to hear from your lips that you're all right and not neck-deep in a mystery.

With love,

A

SHE BARELY CONTAINED her smile at the remainder of his email. Of course he would worry, and yet he knew her so well. Letting out an uncharacteristic, girlish sigh, she leaned back and took another sip of her iced coffee.

Rick had disappeared without a trace and no one knew anything about it. Was it possible that he'd come up here to find CeCe?

THE LUNCH CROWD was thinning when Margot said good-bye to CeCe. She'd looked absolutely exhausted after serving lunch and had told Margot she'd gotten permission from Lela to take a nap in their spare bedroom.

Margot watched now as her friend climbed the stairs, her shoulders slumping. She hadn't had a chance to share the news about Rick with her yet, but she'd also thought it might be better that way. The less CeCe had on her mind now, the better she would sleep during her nap in the safety of the Wilkinsons' apartment.

Her gaze wandered to the staff that was now hustling out of the kitchen to pick up plates to be washed. As the door swung open, she saw a man yelling at a girl—it looked like

Alice, their sweet server from the first night. Then the door swung shut again. She wondered what the matter was. She took a step in the direction of the kitchen just as Alice burst out, a hand wiping away a tear, as she raced past the other workers toward the bathroom. Margot considered intercepting her, but she could clearly see the woman wanted privacy.

Checking her phone, Margot saw that it was getting close to her horseback riding lesson anyway. She sucked in a deep breath and made her way to the front doors. Her questions for the kitchen staff would have to wait. It would likely be better this way since tempers could cool and she could speak with Alice privately about what had happened, using the guise of having seen her flee the kitchen earlier.

Satisfied that she had her next steps in place, she set off for the barn. Before lunch, she'd dressed for the occasion, putting on tall boots she'd borrowed from CeCe, jeans, and a flannel shirt rolled up at the cuffs. She also had a baseball cap on to keep the sun from her eyes. It was warm, the mountain air a bit humid, but she had on a tank top under the flannel should she get too warm.

Several others joined her trajectory as she neared the stables and she was glad to see Jenny among them.

"Where's Ron?" she asked with a forced smile, remembering Jenny's coldness earlier.

"I don't know. He said he'd be here, but..." She looked around and shrugged. "You ever ridden before?"

"Once before. It was a lot of fun. You?"

Just then the instructor came out, calling for them to draw near for the ground rules.

"Uh, no, but it's something to pass the time, you know?" Jenny said and then made her way to where the instructor stood.

Margot thought about Jenny's answer and then looked around, again wondering where Ron was. Weren't they together? Or had she assumed? No, she hadn't. They had clearly been together that first night at the table, though Jenny never truly looked happy around the older man.

When they were done with the instructions, they were each paired up with a horse. Margot's mount was a beautiful buckskin named Sandy. She had a light tan coat, a black mane, and a sweet disposition.

"Hello, girl," she said, crooning to the horse who nudged her palm.

"She's probably looking for a treat," an older man said.

He had on a cowboy hat and boots that looked worn in.

"Didn't he say not to feed them?"

The old man winked and pulled a sugar cube from his back pocket. "I've been coming here since they opened the place. Name's Bubb."

"Bubb?" Margot's eyebrows rose.

The older man laughed. "It's a nickname, but everyone around here knows me by it."

"Nice to meet you, Bubb," she said with a chuckle. "My name's Margot."

"Nice to meet you too," he said, stepping forward and extending a hand toward the horse. "Sandy likes the sugar while my horse, Spirit, is a carrots man himself."

Margot laughed and looked back to where the instructor was helping a shorter woman get on her horse using a stepstool.

"I'm pleading the fifth if he finds out my horse got sugar."

"Don't worry, I'm a friend of Kyle's over there."

Just then Kyle called out and told everyone else to mount up. Margot easily pulled herself up into the saddle and then grasped the horn tightly. She'd forgotten how high up being on a horse was.

At her nervous laugh, Bubb directed Spirit closer. "Don't worry there, Margot. Spirit and Sandy are good friends. I'll stick near ya during the trail ride."

"Much obliged, sir," she said in her best southern accent while tipping her baseball cap toward him.

He laughed and nodded approvingly. They made easy conversation until Kyle directed them toward the trail. Margot noticed that Jenny maneuvered her horse easily behind him, as if she'd been riding for a long time. Maybe Margot had heard her wrong when she said she hadn't ridden before.

They were able to take the path two by two and Bubb rode next to Margot, pointing out things of interest along the path.

"Say, Bubb, you've been up here a bunch, right?" she finally interjected.

"That's right."

"Do people live around here? Like, people not associated with the resort?"

She thought of the faint trail behind CeCe's cabin. Either it was used by guests who got lost, resort staff who wanted to go out into the wilderness, or by someone who lived nearby. Any of those options could be cause for closer inspection if they had anything to do with breaking into CeCe's cabin.

"Nah, can't say as I've ever heard that. Far as I know, the Wilkinsons actually own quite a bit of land up here. They wanted to keep the view unobstructed and what not."

"I see."

"If there was a place to live," he continued, as if not hearing her reply, "my guess is it would be toward the lake. I've heard rumor of a cabin out there, something only the Wilkinsons know about, but you'd have to be an experienced rider to get out there."

"Really? Why?" She was intrigued by his rumor.

"The terrain. I suppose you could walk it, but it would be a lot easier by horseback. You'd just need to be careful because there wouldn't be an exact trail, you know? Trails are either made by man or by beast, but they have to be made."

"So, you're saying someone would have to ride out to the cabin to reach it."

"Exactly. There are no roads that I know of and it wouldn't be a pleasant walk. No, Spirit here'd take you, but it'd be slow going. And that's assuming there even *is* a cabin. I wouldn't put money on it, seeing as how the Wilkinsons stick pretty close to the lodge these days. Used to be a time where—"

He was cut off by the sound of a scream. Then, up ahead, they saw Jenny's horse rear back. She held on tight, her face red with the effort, until the horse came back down, prancing back and forth until Jenny could calm it. Kyle called out that everything was all right.

"Wonder what happened?" Margot mused.

"Snake most likely," Bubb said. "That's Prancer, for obvious reasons. He's a feisty one, but Jenny knows how to handle him."

Margot blinked. "You know Jenny?"

"I wouldn't say *know* her, but I've seen her before, yes. She's a good rider, that one."

Margot merely smiled, her mind whirring with questions as Bubb jumped into a story of horseback riding up in the mountains when he was a boy. Margot only half listened as she tried to figure out a reason that Jenny would have lied about knowing how to ride.

CHAPTER 6

THANKFULLY, DINNER WAS UNEVENTFUL AND WHEN THEY got back to CeCe's cabin, it had been undisturbed.

"Why don't you stay with me again tonight?" Margot suggested. "You should sleep better knowing I'm there. Or I can stay here on your couch."

"Margot, you are *not* sleeping on my couch during your vacation. I won't hear of it. Let me just grab a few things and I'll come back with you. Okay?"

Margot nodded and waited for her friend to put together a small bag of items she'd need. As she waited, she walked to the large windows overlooking the woods. During the day, it was verdant and beautiful, but at night, it was almost spooky. She wouldn't say as much to CeCe, but the reality of the trail she'd found and the fact that things were not adding up here at the resort made matters that much more serious. She only had two more days to figure out what was going on. A thought that made her all the more sure that someone was playing a trick on CeCe. A very cruel trick, but a trick indeed.

For some reason, though it went against logical sense, she didn't think that Rick was behind all of this.

CeCe came back out into the main room with a tote slung over her shoulder and a pair of fluffy pink slippers in her hand. "This should do it."

"I'm glad to see you got the essentials," Margot said with a grin, indicating the slippers.

"A woman needs to be pampered."

Margot laughed and led the way out the front door and to her cabin. The door lock popped open with a soft click and she stepped into the dark room. Flicking on the light, she froze. CeCe bumped into her with a soft *oomph*.

"Margot," she said with impatience.

"CeCe," Margot said in a strained whisper. "Get back."

"Margot, what is it?" Her friend's voice was stern, no longer playful.

"Th-there's s snake in the middle of the room."

With strength Margot didn't know she possessed, CeCe yanked Margot back and slammed the door shut. Her hand trembled on Margot's shoulder. "What did it look like?"

"Uh…" Margot blinked rapidly, the only thought in her mind was the length of brown and tan on the floor coming toward her. All right, so maybe it hadn't been moving but it felt like it. "B-brown. And tan."

"Oh my," CeCe said as they both backed away from the door.

"What? Is that a poisonous snake?"

"Sounds like a copperhead. I don't think they are aggressive, but still, we have to get it out of there!"

"I know," Margot said, wondering if it was too late to simply go back to Cece's place to stay.

"How did it get in there in the first place?" CeCe asked, almost to herself.

Margot's mind snapped to the incident earlier that day. Hadn't Bubb said Jenny's horse had been startled by a snake? And now this. Either the resort was crawling with snakes or…was it possible someone had put it in her cabin?

"I'm calling Chuck," CeCe said, reaching for her phone.

"Why, is he a snake whisperer?"

CeCe rolled her eyes. "No, but he's a man and he grew up in these mountains. Maybe he'll know what to do."

When Chuck arrived with one of the stable-hands, they bravely went into her cabin and, several minutes later, came out with a canvas bag and triumphant smiles.

"Good thing Mike here knows how to deal with snakes. I'm no good, but you ladies should be fine tonight. We checked the rest of the cabin as well—just the one."

Margot felt better and yet, even after their reassurances, she felt uneasy stepping into the cabin, looking around every corner.

"This is ridiculous," CeCe said, shaking her head. "I *hate* snakes."

"I'm not fond of them in the places where I'm going to sleep," Margot said with a smile. But her mind was far from their conversation. Was it possible that someone had placed the snake in the cabin? Had they wanted them to go back to CeCe's cabin to stay for the night? Possibly for the sake of ease? Or was someone trying to scare her? Or was it possible a snake had just found its way into the cabin?

"Has this happened before?" she asked CeCe as the woman pulled her feet up on the couch, still looking around uneasily.

"No. At least not that I've heard of. These cabins are relatively new, and the older ones have been redone recently. I assume they close up holes that snakes could get in, but I suppose there's always a way, right?"

"I suppose," Margot said, though she wasn't convinced.

Setting her mind against worry and fear, she took a deep breath and looked at CeCe. "Let's put it behind us. We'll have tea, chat like the old friends that we are, and go to bed without a worry because they have removed the *only* snake in here."

CeCe grinned at Margot's show of bravado and nodded definitively. "Yes. I agree."

So, for a little while longer, they drank tea and talked about life since they had last seen one another, and then they went to bed, though Margot was sure that they both checked the sheets before crawling in.

CeCe was just leaving the cabin when Margot came out of her room the next morning. She hadn't slept well, dreams of snakes filling her mind and making her toss and turn. Hoping that CeCe had better sleep, she waved to her friend as she closed the door and made her way to the coffee maker. She would still drink a cup of coffee in the dining hall, but there was something about beautiful mornings with a cup of coffee in hand.

Half an hour later when her phone buzzed on the table next to her, she was surprised to see that CeCe had texted. Had she forgotten something in the cabin?

Big meeting. *Hurry!*

THE WORDS DIDN'T QUITE MAKE sense. Was there a meeting for the staff? If so, why would she attend? Either way, she could make her way to the dining room since it was close to breakfast.

Dressing quickly in shorts and a light t-shirt with a striped cardigan for the morning chill, she made her way down the wooded path, her eyes scouring it for snakes now. She arrived at the lodge quickly.

Chuck sat behind the front desk looking harried. Odd, seeing as how it was still early morning and there didn't seem to be many guests in the area. She flashed a smile at him and walked toward the dining hall.

"Oh! Missus Durand, don't—" he said but too late. Margot had already opened the door to see resort staff circled around Detective Sal Rexton, his face a shade of crimson that didn't look healthy.

"I *told* them to keep the door shut until I was ready."

Margot blinked. "I'm sorry. I didn't know."

"You," he said, his eyes narrowing. He strode toward her and the circle of people parted like the Red Sea before Moses. "You found the body with that other woman."

The way he said it made her feel somehow as if she were to blame for the poor man's death. "Yes." She didn't back down. "You took our statements," she said, though she wanted to add that he had also overlooked obvious evidence, but she knew now wasn't the time to point that out.

"I'll need to talk to you again."

She blinked, looking around the circle until she saw CeCe's face, her eyes wide in shock.

He tossed a hand in her direction then charged back to the circle as if he'd dealt with Margot all he needed to. Then he was back to barking orders at the staff and saying how he and his men would be questioning everyone, leaving no stone unturned, and not leaving until he had what he wanted. She felt as if he'd used every cliché in the book but she merely pressed her lips together and waited.

Eventually, he let the staff go and guests began to trickle in. CeCe rushed toward Margot, her eyes as wide as saucers. "I can't believe it, can you?"

"Believe that it's a good thing Detective Rexton didn't become a doctor?"

CeCe frowned. "What?"

"Because he has no bedside manner."

CeCe rolled her eyes. "No. Margot, Darren Stevens was murdered."

"I know."

"What?" CeCe looked shocked.

"I had a feeling," Margot said. "There were a few things that didn't line up with the crime scene and—"

"Margot, he thinks someone here did it."

"Of course he does. Why wouldn't he?"

"But, Margot," CeCe said, gripping her arm, "that means someone here is a murderer."

Margot nodded solemnly. "I know."

One of the wait staff came up at that moment and CeCe was pulled away, but soon the room was filled with guests and Detective Rexton was taking the podium, his pudgy finger tapping loudly on the microphone.

"Is this thing even on?" he said, his voice bellowing out of the speakers. Many in the room responded with angry yeses. Margot noted their coffee cups were empty and had a feeling that was partly responsible for the mood.

"Now listen," Rexton began, his mood matching that of the grouchy morning guests. "We've got a situation here, folks." Murmurs broke out around the room. "There was a man found dead here just the other night."

The audible gasps in the room drew Margot's attention around. She noted that most people hadn't heard about the death since it had happened at night and they'd done a quick job of clearing the scene, likely too quickly in Margot's opinion, but now there was no reason to keep it quiet.

"Upon first look, we assumed accidental death, all of the facts lined up to that, but then as we processed evidence, we found some inconsistencies."

"What does this mean?" a woman on the verge of hysterics said.

"Settle down now," he said, holding up a steadying hand. "Because of this, we will be completing a more thorough investigation. Stan and Lela have graciously offered us the access we need, but what I need from you is your cooperation." He sent his focused stare around the room, as if he could look into the souls of everyone. "We'll do our best not to interrupt your schedule, but we will need statements from you all, to check alibis and the like."

More murmuring broke out. Margot distinctly heard guests frustrated about the interruption of their vacation and she felt sorry for them. But wasn't the investigation of a man's death more important than one's vacation?

"Now, enjoy your breakfast and please pay attention to the deputy that will come around to your table to tell you when and where your statement will be taken."

Margot watched as Rexton stepped down, his stare hard as if he expected opposition. She felt bad for him, knowing he had a difficult job to deal with all of the people who would be unhappy and those who would be frantic and worried for their safety. Despite their first meeting, she wanted to think the best of the detective and hoped everyone would make his job easy.

He passed her without a sideways glance and then she was immersed in the conversation of the table, Fran and Edgar talking in animated tones about how this was the most excitement they'd ever had on a vacation. Margot wasn't sure she'd call this excitement. Murder was never exciting. Though they did have something right--this vacation would be different than any they had ever taken.

CHAPTER 7

MARGOT'S MORNING PASSED WITHOUT CONSEQUENCE, HER meeting with one of the detectives set up for later that afternoon. Then an idea struck her and she made her way toward the kitchen.

"Hello, Missus Durand," Alice said, her dark hair slipping out from the cap around her face. "Can I help you with something?"

Margot smiled, looking guilty. "I was actually wondering if I could possibly get my hands into some dough."

Alice frowned, confused. "What do you mean?"

"I'm a baker," Margot laughed. "I thought CeCe had warned the kitchen staff. She'd told me I could make a little creation for Stan and Lela."

"Oh, how wonderful," Alice said, clasping her hands in

front of her. "She didn't mention it, but I'm sure it would be fine."

"Perfect," Margot said. She felt slightly guilty, thinking that this was the best way for her to get to know the kitchen staff and ask them a few questions about CeCe. It was true, she wanted to bake, but she'd rather know if any of the staff had a desire for CeCe's job more.

"Why don't I show you around?"

"That'd be great. Are you sure I won't be in the way?"

"I'll ask sous chef Alexander, but I don't think so."

Margot followed the girl through the kitchen, first meeting the sous chef, who graciously welcomed her, and then the rest of the staff. They were all exceptionally nice, helpful, and all seemed to love CeCe. When they found out that they went back as friends, the questions seemed endless.

Alice finally showed her to a small workstation and pointed her in the direction of the ingredients she would need.

"This is perfect. Thank you, Alice. You're sure this isn't an inconvenience?"

She laughed. "I'm positive. Besides, Betty does her work early in the morning and then she's off for the rest of the day. She lives down the hill—as those of us who live up here call it. She won't be back until tomorrow anyway."

"Then I'll get to work."

And work she did. Unsure of what the Wilkinsons would like, she decided to do her famous vanilla bean macaroons, a batch of *religieuse*, and éclairs with her famous chocolate adornments to complete the platter she would take to Stan and Lela.

The feeling of flour on her fingers was refreshing and she took longer on her presentation than she normally would have. Just as she was putting on the finishing touches to her *religieuse*, a woman stopped behind her, obviously admiring her work.

"Beautiful," she said, awe lacing her words.

"Thank you." Margot stood up, looking at her work. There were a few imperfections that wouldn't have been an issue had she been in her own kitchen, but she was happy overall with how they had turned out.

"I'm Shelly," the woman said, holding out her hand but, seeing the icing bag in Margot's one hand and the sticky mess on the other, she grinned and dropped it.

"Sorry." Margot shrugged. "I'm Margot. Nice to meet you."

"You too. What are you up to here?" She again observed Margot's work with an appreciative eye.

"I thought the Wilkinsons might like these. I'd promised to bake for them."

"That's nice of you." She turned her gaze up to look at Margot. "Better watch out, they might hire you."

"Oh, I think Mister Wilkinson already tried that, and he hadn't even tried my pastries."

"Sounds just like him. Seems to give anyone a job around here." The bitterness in the woman's voice surprised her. Was this it? Was the woman a possibility for someone who wanted to take CeCe's job? It seemed unlikely that she would be involved in that, her mannerisms speaking more to a tired mother than a woman on the look out to take someone's job, but Margot knew better than to assume.

"What do you mean?" she asked, trying to sound nonchalant and keeping her attention on the pastries.

"I just think that Stan should watch out who he hires. That's all. Not you," she said with a laugh, "you look like you *know* how to do your job."

Yes, there was definitely bitterness in the woman's tone.

"Sounds like you know of someone he's hired that is maybe lacking talent?" Margot looked up at the woman, who merely shrugged.

"Far be it for me to tell him how to do his job, but a kitchen is a difficult place to work. Hard enough without someone coming in who doesn't know what she's doing."

Now Margot's attention was held completely by the

woman. "Oh?" she said, hoping it would merely encourage the woman.

She looked around, careful to make sure no one was nearby. "I don't mean to speak out of turn, but it's just not right. She doesn't have experience for a kitchen like this and he practically dotes on her."

That definition could fit CeCe, but would this woman have stayed for so long if she felt CeCe was incompetent? Not to mention that Margot had worked with CeCe and knew for a fact that she was one of the *most* competent chefs. Margot began to wonder if Shelly would freely admit to who she was talking about or if she'd have to artfully coax it from her.

"You think he's playing favorites?" she said conspiratorially.

"I wouldn't put it past him," Shelly said, crossing her arms over her chest, her white chef's coat pulling taut at the shoulders. "I mean, don't get me wrong, I like Stan and Lela just as well as everyone else but she…" She shook her head. "She's a piece of work. Dropped three plates *just* last night."

Margot had known CeCe to be a bit klutzy in the past, but three plates? That didn't seem right. Then again, they *had* found a dead body and there was the potential that her ex-husband was stalking her. It would be enough to make anyone a little distracted. Still, she was jumping to conclusions.

"I mean, Alice is nice," Shelly continued, as if Margot's silence had been some sort of judgment on her comments. "I really like her, but I don't think she should be working in the kitchen. To go from the front desk, to guest services, to waiting on tables? It's just not logical."

Margot almost breathed a sigh of relief. She didn't get a feeling that Shelly had it out for anyone, but her frustration was evident. Though now that she possibly felt guilty, she had no end of nice things to say about the sweet waitress as well.

"Sorry, you caught me on a bad day. This whole *mess* with Detective Rexton coming in and taking over has us all in a tizzy. I mean, we have to make lunch for a whole extra twenty people or so."

Margot offered her sympathies and promised to clean up her station. Shelly was quick to welcome her to be as messy as she'd like and that they'd have someone take care of it. Then she was off to her next task.

Hearing about the extra workload the kitchen staff had, she decided to help and made a few dozen cookies to give to the workers and officers. She even had enough left over to put out as snacks while people waited for lunch that would likely be late.

All the while, she puzzled over her conversation with Shelly. She had known, or at least suspected, that Shelly wasn't to blame for the terrorizing things happening to her friend, and yet her comments described an anomaly.

Why was Alice in the kitchens? It sounded as if she'd already had a go at many of the different areas of work at the resort and without much luck.

A loud clatter from the other side of the kitchen showed the very woman, her eyes wide and several other staff members looking at her in frustration as a platter of food lay on the ground. Margot took it as her cue to leave, but she puzzled over the facts without being able to make much sense of them.

THE LATE AFTERNOON found her being questioned by a deputy. He was a young man who looked to be in his early twenties and new to the force. During the first few minutes while he took her statement, she learned more about him than he asked questions of her. He was recently engaged, new to the police force, and had just gotten a puppy named Wolf, who was in fact *not* a wolf.

"I-I'm sorry, Missus…" He checked his notebook again. "Missus Durand. I'll admit this is my first time questioning anyone about a m-murder." He wiped sweat from his brow, even though it was cool in the lodge area.

Margot took pity on him. "Don't worry, Deputy Forrester, we all have to start somewhere. My late husband was a detective and I remember him coming home after a particularly hard case one night and telling me he was going to quit."

The young man's eyes widened. "Really? Did he?"

"No," she said with a smile as her thoughts filed back to that night and what Julian had said. "In fact, I had him tell me all about the day—the details he could share, of course —and at the end of it, I told him he'd done the right thing and that he'd go back the next day and do great."

"And what did he say to that?" the deputy asked, leaning forward as if the answer could hold the key to his own anxiety.

"He said I was right and he was a smart man for marrying me." She chuckled and shook her head. "I advise you to talk with your fiancée after you're done with work tonight. Have her give you some perspective, because we all have to start somewhere, no matter what we're doing. Chances are, she'll give you some good insight into who you are and how proud she is of you."

"Gosh," he said, the tips of his ears reddening, "you sure know how to put a fella at ease."

"I'm glad to hear it. Now, how about I tell you what I remember from the crime scene?"

Blinking, it took the man a moment but he was back to his notes instantly and nodding, like he'd suggested it. "That'd be great, ma'am."

She did and watched as he made a note of everything, including her observations about the things that seemed out of place.

"You sure are observant," he said, one eyebrow raised.

"My husband taught me a lot about observation."

"He did a good job." He grinned and looked down. "I think that's all I had for you. You're free to go."

She thanked the young man and rose. Seeing Jenny at the other side of the room near the table where she'd placed the cookies and left-over pastries, she walked toward the young woman. She was almost there when an officer approached her. She gently tapped Jenny on the shoulder, and the girl nearly jumped out of her skin.

"Gah!" Jenny said, the sound reverberating throughout the lodge. "What are you trying to do? Scare me to death?"

"I'm sorry," Margot heard the officer say. "It's just time for you to be questioned."

"Do I have to?" Jenny said, taking another bite of one of the éclairs Margot had made. "It's just, I'm like…" She paused, the pastry dropping from her hand. "Oh my gosh, do these have *milk* in them?"

The officer's eyes went wide. "If it's an éclair, then yes, there's usually a cream filling."

"I-I didn't know," she said, tossing the plate into the trash and grabbing her stomach with her other hand. "I-I'm going to be sick. I'm— I'm really allergic."

Then, as wide-eyed as the officer, Margot watched as Jenny turned and all but ran to the bathroom.

"What's wrong?" she said, as if she hadn't just heard the whole exchange between them.

"Seems that young lady is allergic to milk products. Though why she would have been eating an éclair is beyond me. Doesn't everyone know what's in those?"

"Clearly not," Margot said, her attention wandering in the direction of where Jenny had run.

"Say, you're the woman who made these, aren't you?"

She nodded, pulling her attention away from where Jenny had gone. "I am. I hope that was all right."

"More than," the woman said, pouring herself a refill of coffee.

The act brought something to mind for Margot. The first time she'd met Jenny, she'd been drinking coffee. Margot distinctly remembered her pouring a large amount of cream into it. It was possible it had been a non-dairy creamer…but Margot was almost positive it had just been cream.

"Miss?" the officer said.

Margot blinked and forced a smile. "Sorry, I was distracted for a moment there. What did you say?"

"Just wanted to extend the gratitude of all of the officers here to you. Cookies and coffee, it's really all we need in life." She winked and then picked up her clipboard, obviously looking for the next name on her list since

Jenny was now missing.

The hairs on the back of Margot's neck pricked as if in a sensation of warning. Why had Jenny avoided her interview with the police? Was she afraid of them? Or afraid of what she could contribute to the investigation? But it was unlikely she'd had anything to do with the man's death, Margot and CeCe hadn't been that far behind everyone else leaving. It seemed improbable that Jenny could have been over there without being seen.

Then again, stranger things had happened, and she couldn't be sure. Either way, she felt the need to keep an eye on Jenny.

CHAPTER 8

MARGOT TOOK THE PLATE OF GOODIES SHE'D PREPARED AND made her way past the free-standing Staff Only sign placed in front of the stairs. While she hadn't directly been invited to come up at that moment, Stan *had* said he wanted to try her pastries and she felt as if this was as good a time as any. Especially seeing as how the investigation of Darren Stevens' death was now reopened. There was something about pastries that could ease the burden of the soul, or at least she'd always felt that way.

Careful to make sure the plate was well-balanced in one hand, she raised her other fist to knock but the door opened before her knuckles could connect with the solid surface.

"Oh," she said, blinking and looking up. "Are there cameras out here?"

Lela smiled back at her. "Not up here," she admitted cryptically.

Margot mentally kicked herself for not noticing where they were placed. She had a feeling they must be at the base of the stairs. Why such high-tech security?

"How can I help you, Margot?" Lela asked, poised and charming as always.

"I thought I'd take Stan up on his request for pastries. I hope you don't mind, but CeCe said I could use the kitchen. Is she still up here?"

"No, she left about fifteen minutes ago to start working with the dinner crew. There'll be extra mouths to feed, that's for certain." Lela seemed to lose her train of thought for a moment before regaining it with an elegant smile. "You said you brought pastries? Stan will be pleased. Do come in."

Margot smiled her thanks and followed the woman into the lavish space. She again marveled at the appointments that had no doubt been handpicked by the matriarch of the resort.

"You have such a wonderful eye for design," Margot pointed out.

"I studied interior design in college and fell in love with it. Would you like some iced tea?" At Margot's nod, she turned to the bar to fix the tea. "I had my own agency when I lived in New York years ago, but Stan somehow convinced me to leave it all behind and move to the Blue Ridge Mountains of all places. Can you believe it?"

Margot placed the serving platter on the coffee table and took a seat in one of the faux cow's hide chairs. "I can't. I'm sure it was a shock for you to be up here. I mean…it's beautiful, but decidedly *not* New York."

"My thoughts exactly," she said, bringing over a silver platter with two glasses on it, a lemon wedge atop each glass. "But I've fallen in love with it."

"I'm glad to hear it."

"And what about you? CeCe has told us all about your baking exploits, but what is this I hear about investigations?"

Margot blinked. Where had she heard that? "I, uh…"

"I was curious," Lela said, sipping her tea. "I Googled you."

"And what did you find?" she said with a laugh.

"Several articles from the North Bank Times detailing your hand in solving crimes. Dare I say they follow you?"

Margot swallowed uncomfortably. "I wouldn't say that exactly."

"Of course not, dear," she said, patting Margot's hand. "I was just surprised is all. What do you make of the death of poor Darren? I'm still in shock." She leaned back, her face growing paler by the moment.

"I'm not sure. It seems as if the police are doing a good job—"

"Nonsense. Sal assured us it was an accident only to show up twenty-four hours later saying it was murder. I *do* want to get to the bottom of this, believe you me, but I'm terrified of what it will do to our reputation."

"What can you tell me about Darren?" Margot said.

"Not much. A good man. A bit of a recluse, really. He's lived up in the mountains all his life. We were fortunate to hire him as our groundskeeper. I'm at a loss as to what to do now, but that's not important." She sipped her tea and choose an éclair from the plate, placing it on one of the napkins she'd brought over. "You and dear CeCe found him, didn't you? I've been meaning to come apologize to you for that."

Margot blinked. "Apologize. But why?"

"My dear," Lela said, with all the grace of a southern debutant, "when one's guests find a *dead body,* one finds it necessary to apologize."

"I see." Margot took a sip of her tea, trying hard not to smile. The situation wasn't funny, and yet Lela was just *so* proper.

"Speaking of CeCe," Lela continued, "can you tell me what's gotten in to her? She's never been so...off."

"What do you mean by 'off'?" Margot asked, though she knew exactly what Lela meant.

"She's just not been herself."

At that moment, Stan came through the door, shedding his baseball cap. "Margot!" he bellowed. "What a treat. And oh boy, are those *pastries*?"

She smiled up at the congenial, if not flamboyant, man. "Yes, they are. As promised."

He plopped unceremoniously down next to Lela and reached for the largest *religieuse* on the platter.

"Oh, Stan," Lela said, giving him an admonishing glance.

"What?" he said around a mouthful of the pastry and cream.

She rolled her eyes and looked at Margot. "He's on a diet."

"I'm as healthy as a horse. And this is delicious," he said, wagging his eyebrows.

Margot smiled.

"I was just asking Margot about CeCe, dear. Haven't you noticed her acting differently?"

He nodded, his mouth full.

"Maybe it's just the added stress of the investigation," Margot offered, though feeling a bit guilty because she knew *exactly* what was going on.

"True," Lela said, her gaze sliding into the distance. "But I think it started before that." She looked over at her husband, wiping a bit of cream from the corner of his mouth and offering him a sweet smile before looking back at Margot. "I know it may seem a bit strange—that we are her employers and yet so worried about her—but I feel comfortable telling you this, since you are one of her closest friends."

Margot's heart began to beat faster. What exactly was Lela going to share with her?

"You see," she said glancing at Stan before looking back at Margot, "we love CeCe like she was our daughter." At the word 'daughter,' her voice cracked. "We care for her very deeply and she's been invaluable to us here.

The couple looked at each other for a moment and Margot felt like there was more they wanted to share but they held back.

"I almost forgot!" Stan slapped a hand to his head. "These pastries took my mind off of what I was doing. Lee, we're wanted down stairs. Sal needs us to answer some questions. I'm sorry, Margot. I hate to break up the party."

She smiled and stood. "Not at all. I just wanted to share these with you. Thank you not only for letting me stay here, but for taking such good care of my friend."

"She's been a blessing to us." Lela's eyes glossed over in admiration and Stan wrapped his arm around her.

Margot thanked them and excused herself, but her mind stayed with their conversation. Was it possible that what was happening to CeCe actually had nothing to do with Rick?

~

Margot's mind was spinning with thoughts as she left the Wilkinsons' space, bypassing them as they broke off to talk with Detective Sal. He eyed Margot as she walked past with something close to annoyance, but she ignored it. Instead, she went to find CeCe.

The minute she walked into the dining hall, she knew something was wrong. All staff members had frozen where they were and CeCe stood in the midst of it all, a broken vase and light pink roses scattered at her feet.

Margot took a quick inventory of the staff, but found only Alice was missing, if she'd counted everyone. Then it was as if CeCe was awoken from a spell. She took a step back and a card she'd been holding fluttered to the floor. She blinked rapidly just as Margot's phone began to vibrate. Of all the times to have reception enough to get a call, she thought.

Then, CeCe's eyes only briefly meeting Margot's, she took another step back and shook her head before she ran out of the side door. There was no way the staff hadn't seen her terrified expression. Margot knew something had to be done.

Boldly, she stepped forward and carefully picked up the

card, pocketing it, and then she turned to face the kitchen staff.

"CeCe's been having a bit of a rough time. You all know that we were the unfortunate ones to come across Darren's body and I really think it's affecting CeCe on a deep level." She felt the card in her pocket and looked at the roses. Another supposed *gift* from Rick? Margot wasn't sure what they meant, but she had a feeling it wasn't a good memory. "Besides, she's not a fan of pink," she finished lamely.

"We'll get it cleaned up," one of the busboys said, and the rest of the crowd nodded in agreement, dissipating to their various tasks as if nothing had happened.

Margot made her way to the side door, but turned to look back as Alice came in to the dining hall. She looked pale and...was it possible she looked nervous? Their eyes met for a brief second before the sous chef called out to her and she scurried over to where he stood.

Once outside, Margot pulled the card from her pocket. Careful to hold it by the edges in case there was a way to get prints from it, she read the inscription.

WHY DON'T you love me any more? I'm going to shower you with gifts until you do, Love Bug.

-Rick

MARGOT FROWNED. It didn't sound threatening, and yet it didn't sound positive either. But the most notable thing was the signature. It very clearly said *Rick*.

Then her phone started vibrating again and she pulled it out. Adam.

"Hello?" she said, pausing to stay near the lodge where the signal was strongest.

"I've got some news."

Margot looked down at the note and then let out a light sigh. "What is it? Not good, by the sound of your voice."

"It would seem that Rick Moody has been found."

Margot halted her pacing. "Really?"

"Yes. Coworkers got suspicious when he missed work a few days in a row. But, Margot—" He paused and she heard muffled sounds as if he'd covered the mouthpiece of the phone to answer someone. "Sorry," he said a moment later.

"You've really got this whole suspense thing down, Mister Eastwood."

"It's not good news."

"That he was found?"

"More like *how* he was found."

"Dare I ask?"

"He was murdered, Margot."

She gasped. Rick was dead? She looked at the note again. "Well…that's interesting."

"Margot—" Adam said in a chiding tone.

"No," she was quick to explain. "I say it like that because CeCe just got a note supposedly *from Rick*."

"That's impossible."

"I know." Margot paced back toward the path that led to their cabins, her mind racing through all angles.

"Margot, I—"

A scream echoed out through the forest and Margot yanked her head in the direction it had come from. "I've got to go," she said.

"Margot, what's going on?"

She started racing toward the cabins. She knew that voice, it was CeCe!

"No time to explain," she panted, "I'm going to lose the signal, but CeCe needs me." Then she hung up. She felt guilty doing that to Adam when she knew he would want details, but her friend was in trouble by the sounds of it.

When she was near the cabin, she almost stopped to go back. Should she have gotten one of the many police officers and volunteers in the lodge? But by that time, she was already too far to go back.

She raced to the front door only to find it wide open. "CeCe," she called out, taking the steps two at a time and skidding to a stop at the door. CeCe stood just inside the door, every part of her trembling. Margot gently reached out and touched CeCe's shoulder but she yanked away, as if shocked.

"It's me, CeCe, it's Margot."

As if coming out of a trance, CeCe blinked. "Marg—" Then she gave into tears and dropped her head onto Margot's shoulder. "It's horrible. So horrible."

Margot comforted her friend and looked in through the open door. There, propped up behind the couch, was a painting Margot remembered seeing in CeCe's apartment when they had only been out of college for a few years. If she remembered correctly, it had been painted by CeCe's father.

But now, the fact that it was art was the last thing anyone would notice about it. It had been painted over in what looked like blood with two words: *Love me.*

Margot shivered, pulling CeCe closer. "I'm sorry, my friend."

"But...how?" she managed against Margot's shoulder. "How is it here? It was in my storage facility that no one knew about. And is that *blood*?"

Margot squeezed her friend's shoulders and then gently

eased away. "I don't know, but we'll get to the bottom of this. I promise you!"

Though, even as she said it, she began to wonder just *how* they would do that.

Careful not to disturb anything else, Margot made her way toward the painting. The closer she got the more she felt as if the red *did* look like blood. After Adam's news about Rick, she was beginning to wonder what was really going on here.

Was it about CeCe? Or was this about something else entirely?

Either way, she knew what had to happen next, and she had a feeling CeCe wasn't going to like it.

CHAPTER 9

"No," CeCe said, adamantly shaking her head. "I can't. It's not right to burden them with my troubles."

"Would you rather we talk to Detective Rexton? Because, at this point, I think that's our next option. I mean, if this is real blood, we really should involve the authorities."

"I told you last night," CeCe said, pacing back to the window and then turning to look at Margot. "I don't want the police involved yet. Lela and Stan already have so much to deal with and I would only be adding on issues with this whole Rick thing."

Margot's stomach clenched. She still hadn't told her friend about her husband's death. It hadn't been the right time last night, though Margot had felt the pressure to tell her what Adam had discovered. After they'd found the painting, they'd again both spent the night in her cabin. They had decided to come back over that morning to look at it again in the light of day, though it was just as frightening.

"CeCe, I'm afraid I have some…bad news."

Her friend pulled her attention away from the ruined painting and looked at Margot. "What?"

"I was going to tell you last night, but the timing wasn't right. I talked with Adam about what was going on here—"

"I asked you not to share," she said, looking hurt that her friend had broken her trust.

"I know, but I haven't mentioned anything to Stan or Lela, I just needed to have his perspective on this because he has connections I don't have."

"What did he say?" she asked, looking weary.

"He was concerned at first, of course, and looked into where Rick might be. He found out that he had disappeared about two weeks ago."

CeCe's eyes widened. "Right when I started being harassed by him again."

"I found that strange as well. Anyway, I told him to keep looking and he did." She hesitated, knowing the next part would be difficult as well as confusing to her friend. "But, CeCe, Adam told me last night that Rick was found…dead."

"D-dead?" CeCe paled. "You…you're wrong. He can't be

dead. He's tormenting me—clearly, he's not dead. He-he can't be."

"I know it seems impossible, but Adam wouldn't have told me if it weren't true. CeCe, he was murdered."

CeCe backed away from the painting and toward a chair across the room. She sunk down, dropping her head to her hands. "Margot, what is going on?"

Margot came to her side, perching on the edge of the chair and resting her hand on her friend's back, rubbing in a soothing manner. "I'm sorry, CeCe. I know this isn't what you wanted to hear—murder never is—but it does give us some insight."

"Insight?" She looked up at Margot through tear-filled eyes.

"Yes. Because it's clearly *not* Rick who is stalking and tormenting you, that means there's something else behind this."

"But what?" Her friend's voice broke with the emotional strain. "I have no idea why anyone would single me out this way. I haven't done anything to *anyone*. I'm a good worker, a good friend—at least I hope so—and I keep to myself most of the time. I haven't even said an unkind word here at work. There is literally *no one* who would have any reason to harm me like this."

Margot had already gone through these things mentally before CeCe had even summarized them and she had to agree, it made no sense why CeCe was the target of someone's cruel games. And yet she was.

"I don't know. Sometimes people latch on to something they see in someone. Maybe you're a surrogate for someone else's anger. Or maybe it's not about you..." Margot's mind began to fill in possible ideas as she'd done before. She'd vetted most of the kitchen staff and had a feeling her gut reaction was true there. No one wanted to oust her from her job.

So there had to be something else. If it truly wasn't related to CeCe as a person, then possibly her position at the resort? But that seemed difficult to believe considering the reality that CeCe was just a chef. A talented one, of course, but still nothing more special than that.

"We need to talk to Lela and Stan."

CeCe let out a huge sigh and slowly nodded. "I suppose you're right."

They left the cabin, securing the door behind them though it felt futile since it was obvious whoever had placed the painting as well as the other items in her room had special access.

Margot again reminded herself that she needed to find a way to access the logs for entry into the cabins. It made the most sense that a maid's keycard had been stolen, but when she'd suggested that to CeCe, her friend had said there hadn't been any reports of a theft or a missing card.

They walked through the lush, tree-lined path toward the lodge and, as soon as they entered, CeCe went to talk to the young woman behind the desk, informing her that the maids were to skip CeCe's room.

Then they made their way up the stairs to the Wilkinsons' residence.

Before CeCe could knock, Stan was at the door. "There's my CeCe girl," he said, welcoming them in and kissing CeCe on the cheek. "What brings you our way so early in the morning?"

"I'm sorry to interrupt," she said, glancing between Stan and Lela still in a white robe at the small dinette table. "There's something I must tell you both."

They looked concerned but Stan ushered them to the table and made sure they both had steaming mugs of coffee before she could begin.

"Come now, dear," Lela said, her smile matching the warmth of the cup between Margot's hands. "Tell us what is the matter."

With a steadying breath and a glance at Margot for encouragement, CeCe plunged into the story of what had happened. The Wilkinsons were quiet through it all, though a look of horror came over them as CeCe explained the multiple 'gifts' the admirer had left her, ending with the last one.

"Blood?" Lela said, her features paling. "This is very serious."

"I know," CeCe said, dropping her gaze. "Margot encouraged me to tell you both about this. I should have told you before, but I didn't want to add to your burden. There's already so much going on."

"Nonsense," Stan said, slapping the table. "We care about you, CeCe girl, you're not just another employee to us. You're like family. You should be able to come to us for anything. Can you remember that?"

She offered a sheepish smile. "I can."

"Good," he said with finality. "Now, we need to figure out what to do."

"I think we need to involve the police," Margot said, speaking up for the first time.

"Margot," CeCe said, sending her an admonishing look. "If they get involved, it'll only mean more grief for us all here. I think you're more than qualified to figure out who's bothering me."

"But the police—"

"Will only get in the way." CeCe's look implored Margot to see things her way.

"But the blood."

"It's probably only paint."

"And the snake—that was a serious threat."

"It was in *your* room, and we have no evidence that it was placed in there. It could have found a way in through the vents."

Margot was beginning to feel frustrated. Didn't her friend see that cases of stalking like this were a serious thing? Didn't she see the potential danger? Besides, there was also the reality that *if* the blood *was* real on the painting, it would be serious cause for alarm. And, depending on whose blood it was, it could be part of an ongoing investigation. Though, her hunch was just that—a hunch that the blood would prove to be Rick's.

"Please, Margot, see things my way. I don't have anyone to accuse so a restraining order isn't possible. There's been no real damage to me, so I can't point to that. The only things are the threatening notes."

"And the blood—"

"You mean the paint."

They stared at each other for a long moment before Margot nodded. "All right. Okay. I've already told you that I would look into this, that hasn't changed, but if *anything* else happens that seems to involve blood or a direct threat to your life, we go to Detective Rexton and tell him everything."

"Yes," CeCe agreed.

Margot and CeCe left Stan and Lela to the peace of the

early morning, but Margot couldn't help but feel as if she'd agreed to something very dangerous.

AFTER BREAKFAST, Margot stopped to talk with Fran and Edgar for a few minutes before making her way through the lingering crowd toward the lodge entry. She was going to talk to the girl behind the desk about the entry logs, something she'd forgotten to ask Lela and Stan about getting access too, when she spotted a familiar silhouette across the room. No, it couldn't be.

Her eyes narrowed and, as the door closed and cut back on the sunlight, Adam's face came into focus. It *was* Adam!

She picked her way through the crowd toward him, coming to stop in front of him, breathless. "You're here. How are you here?"

"What kind of greeting is that?" he asked with a grin.

She went up on her tiptoes to place a kiss on his cheek then looked him in the eye again. "Why are you here?"

"For a long overdue vacation, of course. Don't I get to take one too?"

Her hands found their way to her hips of their own accord. "Why are you really here?"

"Vacation," he said with another wide grin.

"I don't believe you."

He shrugged, trying his best to look innocent. "Vacation… and the possibility of helping you."

"Ha! I knew it." She narrowed her eyes. "Does the chief know you're here?"

"He knows I went on vacation." Adam turned his gaze up to survey the room around them. "And I may or may not be working with Les on Rick Moody's death."

"So Les knows you're here."

"Of course, he's my partner. He was more than happy to see me go on vacation."

Margot rolled her eyes. "You are ridiculous. You're here to help me find out who's bothering CeCe, aren't you? And to tell me the details of Rick's death. And to—"

"Woah, hold on there. I can't divulge details of an ongoing investigation."

"Well, can you send a sample back to the lab to test for a match with Rick's blood?"

He frowned. "Rick's blood. What are you talking about?"

"Last night," she began, but Adam cut her off.

"You mean when you almost gave me a heart attack when you hung up on me?"

"I'm sorry about that. CeCe was screaming and—"

"Why was she screaming?"

"Because of the painting. And the blood."

"Back up, will you?"

Margot grinned despite the situation. She had missed this man and his humor, but also his hyper-focus. When there was something to be analyzed or studied, he was the first to focus and get to business.

"Come here," she said, pulling him toward a couch in the far corner. Then she told him everything.

When she was done, he shook his head and whistled low. "Margot, we should talk to the local authorities."

"I know, that's what I told CeCe, but she's bound and determined not to. There's already the death investigation going on and—"

"What?"

Margot pressed her lips together and shook her head. How had so much have happened in such a short amount of time? She quickly filled Adam in on what had happened, how they had come across the body, and the incongruities she had noted when they'd ruled it an accident. Then she explained how Detective Rexton had come back, establishing it a homicide.

"That explains all of the squad cars outside," he said, nodding.

"Yes, but when I told CeCe to involve him, she doesn't want to prolong the investigation here for the sake of the

Wilkinsons. She has a bit of a point though with the fact that, while she's been threatened, there is no one attached to the acts."

"So, you think the blood on the painting could be Rick's."

"After what you told me last night—that he was dead—I'm beginning to wonder if someone went to great lengths to research Rick and his previous stalking habits toward CeCe. Then, maybe when he got in the way or wouldn't give the information they needed, he had to be…removed."

"You mean killed."

"Yes. Whether by accident or initially, I think they may have taken that opportunity to get some of his blood."

"It's a bit of a stretch, Margie," he said, using her familiar nickname.

"I know. I'm at the hypothesizing stage where anything goes," she said with a sad smile. "Even murder."

Adam nodded thoughtfully. "All right. I'll take a sample of the blood and send it off to the lab. If they find that it *is* Rick's, though, we'll be obligated to call in the local authorities, not to mention my team."

"I understand, and CeCe and the Wilkinsons will have to understand too."

He nodded and stood. "Why don't you show me around

and then take me to the painting? We've got some serious work to do."

Margot nodded her agreement, a subtle feeling of peace washing over her at the reality that she was no longer alone. She'd always had CeCe, but her friend was hurting as well as inexperienced in investigation. With Adam there, Margot felt certain they could get to the bottom of it all.

CHAPTER 10

AFTER A LONG DAY OF MAKING CALLS, GOING TO THE LOCAL post office to overnight the blood sample to the lab, and taking a relaxing stroll through the trees where Margot spent the entire time hypothesizing about the case, the two found themselves back at the lodge for dinner.

"I don't feel like we got anywhere," she admitted as they wound their way through the tables.

"Just be patient. The extended weekend's not over yet, there's still time. I have a feeling we'll get our big break soon."

She cocked an eye at his enthusiasm, but she wasn't so sure she felt it herself. She was scheduled to stay one more day at the resort. One more day to figure everything out. It was impossible. Though she had a feeling the Wilkinsons would gladly let her stay, she wasn't sure she could leave her shop closed for that long. Not to mention the fact that she missed getting her fingers in the dough and being covered in flour all the time.

She thought of her assistant Dexter Ross and how he'd taken a leave of absence. She wondered how he was doing and when he would be able to come back. She often worried about him, knowing the circumstances that led to him leaving were vague and a little frightening to say the least, but Adam assured her that he was all right and that she shouldn't worry. Something easier said than done.

The reality was, she not only missed his help, but his effervescent personality and easygoing manner. And, though she'd never admit it to his face, she missed his experiments. The good, the bad, and even the ugly.

"Margie?" Adam said, bending down to look her in the eye.

"Sorry," she said, blinking. "I was in another place."

"Clearly," he said, chuckling. "Is this our table?"

She looked up to see Sarah and Matt chatting on one side of the table while Fran fussed with the top button of Edgar's polo shirt. Ron and Jenny weren't there yet, but she saw them making their way through the crowd as well. "Yes, this is us."

"Hi, everyone," Adam said, sitting down at the table. "I'm Adam."

His greeting was followed by welcomes all around just as

Ron and Jenny joined them. Conversation was interrupted by a waitress bringing their salads to them, but soon everyone was chatting again.

"So what do you do?" Matt asked Adam.

Margot looked at him to see what he would say.

"I'm a police officer," he said with a smile.

"You don't say," Edgar said, nodding approvingly.

Margot caught the look Jenny shot Adam before looking down and slicing into her dinner roll. Was it fear?

"Are you with the local police?" Sarah inquired, looking at him over her raised phone.

"No. I'm just up for a little rest and relaxation."

"You picked a pretty companion for your vacation," Edgar said and then winced when Fran slapped him.

"Don't pry, Ed."

"It's all right," Adam said in his congenial manner. "Margot is my girlfriend. I was fortunate enough to get a cabin near hers on the other side of the resort. Where are you all staying?"

And just like that, he was gaining information on them all. Margot marveled at the way he did it, asking innocent questions that allowed people to divulge important things about themselves. Things he no doubt stored away for later.

He was a true detective, something she admired about him.

Dinner went smoothly until dessert was announced. Their waitress gave everyone two options: chocolate cake or an ice cream sundae. Margot put in her order for the cake but, as the waitress went around the table, she was shocked when Jenny ordered the sundae. Hadn't she said she was allergic to milk?

"You must have remembered your pills," Margot said with a smile.

Jenny frowned. "What are you talking about?"

"Oh, I thought you had a lactose allergy."

"No," she said with a disgusted look. "I don't know what you're talking about."

Margot wanted to remind her exactly when and where she'd heard that, but the conversation shifted before she could.

"Margot," Adam said later, leaning in so only she could hear him. "You're brooding."

She smirked. "Am not."

"Am too. What's up with you and Miss Snooty over there?"

"I don't trust her, Adam," Margot said, keeping her gaze on Jenny, who was scowling at something Ron had said. "She's lying."

"About?"

"Being lactose intolerant."

Adam laughed, drawing the attention of the table. He raised a hand. "Sorry, folks. Margie here has a great sense of humor."

They all went back to their individual conversations while she shot daggers at Adam with a dark glance.

"Sorry. You were saying?"

"I just mean that she blatantly lied to an officer yesterday about being lactose intolerant and now she's here having an ice cream sundae and says she doesn't know what I'm talking about."

"Maybe she doesn't like to talk to the police."

"Or maybe she has something to hide."

Adam's eyebrow rose and he slowly nodded. "What did you say her name was?"

"Jenny Blane."

"Okay, I'll have Les check her out."

"Thanks." Margot smiled at him and then reached out her fork to take the cherry off the top of his sundae. "I know you don't like these."

He laughed as she ate it. "Very astute of you, Watson."

"Sherlock," she corrected.

∾

AFTER DINNER, Margot convinced CeCe to stay in the lodge with them to play a game of cards. By the end of the night, CeCe was smiling, laughing as if there wasn't the weight of a stalker resting on her shoulders. Margot was thankful for the moment, knowing that it wouldn't last for long but happy that they'd had it.

When the decks of cards had been shuffled and put back, they all headed back to their cabins. As Adam had so astutely pointed out to those at their table that night, he'd gotten the cabin directly next to CeCe's.

"I'm glad you came, Adam," CeCe said. "Margot's done nothing but talk about you and—"

"I have not," Margot said indignantly.

Adam and CeCe shared a boisterous laugh as Margot feigned indifference.

"No, but in all seriousness, she has said how amazing of a detective you are. I'm glad that we can have you here."

"You do know that I think we should go to the police with all of this, right?"

CeCe nodded. "I know, and I almost went up to Detective Rexton today, but every time I got near him, he looked like a tea kettle ready to blow. That vein popping up on his forehead is like a warning sign. I'm afraid he'll either discredit me, discount me, or laugh at me."

"Any good detective would take the time to hear out your story."

"And you have," she said with a gentle smile. "I promise, if anything...*else* happens, we can involve the local authorities."

Margot had a feeling her friend had been about to say if anything *worse* happens, but she couldn't be sure. Would that be the case? Something worse than threatening notes, poisonous snakes, and bloody paintings was difficult to imagine.

They arrived at CeCe's door. "I'll be right next door. And don't worry. I took care of the painting. Once we're sure that it's not related to Rick's death, we'll get it cleaned up for you."

"Thank you," she said, tears sparkling in her eyes. "Good night."

They watched her walk down the path and disappear into the cabin. "So far so good."

"I checked it earlier today. As far as I could tell nothing had been disturbed."

"Well, I suppose that's good. But what's bothering me is the fact that *someone* has access to her cabin." Margot went on to explain the security locks and the way the computer system had been set up.

"Sounds like whoever made that knew what they were doing. That's a great system. Now we'll just need to get our hands on readouts of who has had access to her room."

"And mine," Margot added.

"You still think the snake is part of this?"

"I do," she said. "It was too much of a coincidence. Plus, CeCe was staying in my room, so it makes sense that the snake would have been to frighten us both."

"So you think someone is watching you then?"

As if his statement could bring out eyes from the dense and dark forest surrounding them, Margot looked around before answering. "I do."

She thought of the trail behind CeCe's cabin and how she'd seen Matt coming down the path from there. Was it possible she'd caught him coming from scouting out CeCe's cabin? Or worse, breaking into her cabin?

"Don't worry," Adam said, as if her distracted look had caused him to think she was nervous. "I'll be close by."

"Thank you," she said, squeezing his hand. "Now go get some sleep. We have a case to solve tomorrow."

He kissed her on the cheek and watched as she walked to her cabin, making sure she was safely inside before he turned back to his.

Margot got ready for bed, slipped into her covers—after first checking for snakes—and then lay there staring at the ceiling. The information she'd gathered that day with

Adam filled her mind. No one in the kitchen staff, now interviewed a second time with Adam, had any motive to want CeCe's job. The initial thought that Rick was behind everything was false, but they had spent a few hours going over how someone could know all of the things that they did about CeCe.

The end result was simple. Study. Someone had studied CeCe, and maybe even Rick too. It was also possible that the same person responsible for killing Rick was the same person who was now tormenting his ex-wife.

Margot rolled over on her side, but sleep still wouldn't come. Finally, after one in the morning, she stood and made her way to the kitchen, feeling thirsty. She desperately wanted to sleep, but at the same time, her friend was counting on her to solve this mystery and they were running out of time.

She'd just turned off the tap when a flash of light drew her attention. She hadn't turned on the lights, being able to maneuver by the dim light from the waning moon, so the flash had been easily visible out of the large windows toward the back of her cabin.

Staying in the shadows, she crept to the window and waited. Sure enough, a few moments later, another flash went off, this time closer to CeCe's cabin. It only took her a moment to decide what she was going to do. Rushing back to her room, she pulled on pants and a dark sweatshirt over her pajama top, and slipped into a pair of running shoes. Then, taking her small flashlight with her, she crept out the backdoor and into the trees at the edge of the clearing beside her cabin.

Her footsteps up until that point were quieted by the damp grass, but now she had to watch where she stepped for fear of treading on a branch that would give away her position.

She slipped into the darkness and crept closer to CeCe's cabin. No lights were on and it looked as if Adam's cabin was the same way. When she neared the spot where she'd located the trail before, she paused, slowing her breathing so she could listen.

The regular sounds of the night grew louder as the insects she'd disturbed reemerged and joined in their song again. Then she heard it--the snap of a branch. The sweeping sound of the brush being pushed aside. Someone was coming.

Her heart pounded in her chest and she wished she had some form of defense. Then again, her Krav Maga skills would come in handy, as long as she could see her opponent. Nervously, she turned to look behind her when a *woosh* accompanied hands that shoved her to the ground.

The shattering sound of glass breaking and a cry broke the stillness of the night. As if he'd been waiting for this, Adam's light burst on and moments later, his backdoor flung open. Margot hurried to stand just as her assailant rushed past her and into the dense brush on the small trail she'd found.

"Adam, over here!" she cried out.

He raced toward her. "Margot, are you all right?"

"He went into the woods. Here!" She thrust her flashlight into his hand. "I'll check on CeCe."

When he saw that she was all right, he rushed past her and into the woods, the sound of cracking branches and crashing following him.

Margot turned and ran toward the house, calling out for CeCe.

"I'm okay," her friend replied, the sound of falling glass accompanying a cry of pain.

"Be careful, CeCe!"

"I am," she said, finally opening the backdoor. "The glass is everywhere."

The back-porch light came on and Margot saw her friend standing there, her hands cut and bleeding, as well as her feet.

"Oh, CeCe!" Margot cried out, rushing up the steps to catch her just as she fell into a fit of tears.

CHAPTER 11

"This has to stop," Stan said, pacing back and forth in the medical cabin while CeCe's wounds were bandaged.

"I tried to follow him, but he was too fast." Adam, looking like he'd not only run through the forest but brought most of it back with him, stood brooding with his hands on his hips. Margot knew he hated losing a suspect. "He definitely knew his way around this place."

"I found this attached to a brick," Margot said, holding up a note. "It says, 'If I can't have you, no one can.' I'd say this has taken a turn for the worse."

Margot watched as Lela, her hand resting lightly on CeCe's shoulder, shared a look with Stan. "Maybe you should go to town for a few days, CeCe?" she said, her voice soft and reassuring. "We'll pay for a hotel for you. It could be like a retreat." Lela tried to sound positive, but no one really felt reassured by her words.

"No, I'll stay here. I won't be scared away."

"But, CeCe…" Margot met her friend's gaze. "It could become more dangerous than a brick thrown through your window."

"But if I leave, doesn't that mean they win?"

It was an odd way to look at it, but it did give Margot some perspective. Who was to gain if CeCe left? Certainly not Lela and Stan, they would be out a head chef. The kitchen staff would just be short-staffed, so that wasn't a bonus.

From Margot's standpoint, no one would gain anything.

"We really should involve the police," Adam said.

"But we are," Stan said. "You're here, aren't you?"

Adam grimaced. "Yes, but unofficially."

"But you're here. And you're involved," CeCe said. "That should be enough for now."

Margot wasn't sure why her friend was so adamant against the police being involved, but it was beginning to create an issue. What would happen if something worse happened to CeCe? Would Adam be brought up on charges for not bringing this to Detective Rexton's attention?

"Look, while we wait, I was wondering if I can have access to this database that stores all the information about the access points to the cabins." Adam's request surprised

Margot and he caught her look. "It's doubtful that I'll be able to get back to sleep tonight, so I might as well do something helpful."

"Come with me," Stan said. "I'll show you."

Margot watched them go as Lela continued to rub CeCe's back. "I'm so sorry about all of this, dear. I wish..." She trailed off, but her tone drew Margot's attention. Did she know more about this than she was letting on? But it appeared she loved CeCe almost like she was her own daughter. Margot couldn't imagine her doing anything to her CeCe.

"It's all right. I just wish we could do something to stop this."

They waited as the medic finished cleaning up the wound. He was a young man who mainly worked as a lifeguard but did nursing duties when necessary. He had already promised to keep the night's events confidential so as not to worry the other staff.

"She'll stay with us tonight," Lela said, then turned to the young man. "Could you help her up the stairs and then give her something to help her sleep?"

He nodded in affirmation and, as they watched them ascend the stairs to the Wilkinsons' apartment, Lela rested her hand on Margot's arm. "I don't think I can sleep just now. Should we see what the gentlemen have discovered?"

Margot agreed and they went to the lodge's lobby. Adam sat at the desk with Stan standing behind him, arms crossed.

"This is bizarre, Margot," Adam said, his brow furrowed in concentration.

She stepped around the desk so he could show her what he meant as Stan stepped away to join Lela on the other side.

"First of all, this system is brilliant. Totally state of the art and something I think more companies—especially hotels —should look into. Time stamps, card numbers, access points. It's all here."

Margot looked at the rows of numbers and the highlighted times. "What am I seeing here?" she asked, pointing to the highlighted portions.

"These are times that CeCe's room was accessed. But see here--" He indicated a note on the top of her cabin's account, which opened in a new window. "It says that her cabin was 'restricted'."

"What does that mean?" she asked, looking at Stan and Lela.

"It means that she had requested for her cabin not to be cleaned by our staff."

Margot nodded. "Yes, she requested that yesterday because she didn't want the maid to find the painting."

"But this was enacted weeks ago."

"Weeks?" Margot frowned. "How is that possible? Her cabin has been clean every time we've gone in there."

"Someone must be doing the cleaning," Adam surmised. "See these numbers here? Though her cabin is restricted, there is an access point every morning around ten or so when all of the other maids are on the opposite end of the resort."

"You mean someone is accessing her cabin when she's not there? And it's not a maid?" Lela said.

"Exactly."

"Whose code is it?"

Adam shook his head. "It's not linked to an active profile."

"Active?" Margot asked.

"Yes, the access card is registered to an inactive janitorial account that was last used four years ago."

"F-four, you say?" Lela asked.

When Margot looked up, she noticed how pale Lela had turned. What was making her so uncomfortable?

"Dear," Stan said, drawing her close with an arm around her. "It's late. You should go to bed."

"But—" She looked up at Stan as if she wanted to question him, but then thought better of it. "Yes, I suppose you're right. I-I am tired now."

She disappeared up the stairs. As Margot watched her go, an uneasy feeling sunk into the pit of her stomach. Was it possible Lela was hiding something? She definitely acted suspicious.

"Is it possible a former employee is doing this? Coming back to the resort for some reason?"

"We always deactivate any cards that are left over once someone is terminated from the premises. None of our employees have held grudges. We treat everyone very well. It's highly unlikely it would be one of them."

Margot noticed the way he shifted on his feet and rubbed the tip of his nose. They were blatant signs that he was lying, yet she wasn't sure what he was lying about. The fact that none of his employees had held grudges, or the fact that it was unlikely it could be one of them. Did he have someone in mind?

She was about to ask when Stan let out a huffed breath. "I'm going to go join Lela and CeCe in the apartment. Please, try and get some sleep. Adam, you know how to log out?"

Adam nodded and they both watched him go. Margot wondered if Adam had the same feeling about the Wilkinsons as she did--that they were hiding something.

AFTER A LONG, mostly sleepless night, Margot found the

loud, booming voice of Detective Rexton to be more grating than it had been before. He stood in front of the breakfast crowd all but shouting at the fact that they were close but still hadn't found the killer, then assuring them all that they would.

He continued on and Margot resisted the urge to get up and walk out, but then suddenly he threatened everyone not to leave and turned his attention to CeCe, who had joined Margot's table, bandages covering her palms and making work impossible.

"I need a word, Miss Baxter," Rexton said.

CeCe looked to Margot then back to the detective and nodded, standing to follow him out of the room to the corner table he'd commandeered for his second round of questioning.

"What do you think that was about?" she asked Adam.

"Not sure. Could be that he's got some follow-up questions."

"We both found the body. Wouldn't he call me over as well?"

"He may," Adam said, munching on a crispy piece of bacon, "but he would probably do that separately."

Margot waited a few more minutes and then, after checking her watch, leaned over to Adam. "I'll be back in a few minutes."

He watched her as if she should ask him to join her but, when she didn't, he leaned back and nodded, picking up his coffee.

She slipped out of the lodge and made her way toward her cabin, being careful to slip into the tree line the closer she got. She checked her watch again and nodded, taking up a place behind a large tree trunk that afforded her a view of CeCe's cabin.

Sure enough, at almost ten o'clock exactly, someone slipped down the path wearing the uniform of a maid and carrying a bucket of cleaning supplies. Margot took in the uniform and noticed that the woman wore the wrong shoes. All of the maids at the resort were issued the same shoes, or at least Margot had observed that to be true for the women she'd encountered. This woman was wearing black tennis shoes rather than white.

She paused at the door and, just when Margot thought she would go inside, leaving Margot to guess who it was, the woman turned and surveyed the area behind her.

"Jenny," Margo whispered. Her blonde ponytail swished as she turned back toward the door and slipped inside.

So, Jenny was the one cleaning CeCe's cabin. But why? What in the world did she gain by cleaning it, aside from access to the cabin? Was it possible she was the one terrorizing CeCe?

But that didn't fit. She was a guest at the resort—when she wasn't playing a maid—and had nothing to gain by stalking CeCe. That was the crux of the situation; no one seemingly had anything to gain by CeCe's pain. Unless that was the end in and of itself.

Then again, there were much worse things that could have happened to her friend. The events surrounding her stalking seemed to revolve around forcing her to leave under the guise of her ex-husband being her stalker.

Margot shook her head and left, knowing that it would take Jenny almost an hour to clean the cabin. Part of her wanted to send the police over to catch her in the act, but something told Margot that it wouldn't do any good to stop her; that there had to be someone else behind it. Now she desperately needed to know more about Jenny.

As Margot neared the lodge and was about to slip through the side door that led to the dining hall where she expected to find Adam still, Alice came out, tears flowing down her cheeks.

"Alice, what's the matter?"

The girl sniffed, the sound loud and grating, trying to compose herself. "I-I'm sorry, M-Missus Durand. I'm fine."

"Clearly you're *not* fine. What's wrong?"

As if all she needed was the permission to do so, the girl broke down into more tears and a sniffly explanation of what had happened. Most of what Margot could catch involved a few broken dishes and a lot of yelling from her superior in the kitchen.

"I-I'm sorry. I shouldn't have said all of that. I just… sometimes I think I'm not good at anything."

"Oh, don't say that," Margot said, wrapping a comforting arm around the girl. "I'm sure there are lots of things you're good at."

"Sure, I can sing, but that doesn't do me *any* good here at the lodge." She let out a tired sigh and shook her head. "If it weren't for Uncle Stan, I don't know that I'd still be working here."

"Uncle?" Margot repeated.

"Oops!" Her eyes widened. "I'm not supposed to call him that, seeing as he's my boss and all. You're just so easy to talk to."

Margot smiled at the girl. "So they offered you a job here?"

"Yeah." She wiped the tears from her cheek with her sleeve. "When Chris left, they had an opening and asked me to fill it."

Margot frowned. "Chris?"

"Oh, yeah, sorry—I forgot you wouldn't know who that is. He's my cousin."

"Stan and Lela have a son?" Margot asked.

"Yeah, but he's a bit of a wild one. He's been gone from the resort for a long time now. Had a falling out with my aunt and uncle."

"Over what?"

"I don't know. Whatever parents and kids fight over, I guess. It totally ruined Lela for a while. Stan was just angry. But then they met CeCe. She's really become like the daughter they never had. Rumor in our family is that they are going to have her inherit the resort."

Margot's eyebrows shot up. Did CeCe know about this? Had she purposefully not told Margot or was it that she didn't know it was a possibility? This, if nothing else, was a *large* motivation for her to be a target for the attacks.

"Please don't say anything," Alice pleaded. "I'm also known as the blab in our family and I'll have no end to problems if they know I told you."

"I understand," she said, though in the back of her mind, the need for a conversation with the Wilkinsons increased in importance.

"Thanks for this, Alice, and have you considered asking your aunt and uncle if you could offer some music at night after dinner?"

Alice's eyes lit up. "That sounds like a great idea. Thanks, Missus Durand."

"Call me Margot," she said. "And good luck. Sometimes it

takes us several years before we find things that we're really good at."

The girl smiled back at her as Margot slipped into the dining room. Adam was gone so she made her way to the lodge area where the first thing she saw was CeCe, balling her eyes out in front of Detective Rexton.

"What is going on?" Margot said, coming over to them and staring down at the detective.

"He-he thinks that *I* had something to do with Darren's death."

Margot gave the detective a withering look. "You can't honestly think that. *We* found the body. Besides, she was in the kitchen all day with multiple witnesses. How could she have had the time to go out, overpower a man as big as Darren Stevens, and then make it back in time to walk with me to her cabin only to find him?"

"Calm down, Missus Durand," Rexton said, his natural frown deepening. "I'm not accusing her. We received an anonymous tip and I'm required to flesh it out."

"A tip?" Margot's mind began to spin. Was the person responsible for terrorizing CeCe stepping up their approach by blaming her for something she didn't do?

"Yes. Now, if you'll excuse us, we're having a conversation."

"It'll be all right, CeCe," she said, squeezing her friend's shoulder to convey her support. "We'll get to the bottom of this. Besides, you have nothing to fear because you have nothing to hide." It stood out to Margot that that wasn't fully true, but in the moment, it was the best thing she could think to share.

CeCe nodded, wiping her tears, and Margot turned and walked directly to the other side of the room and up the steps. She had to talk with the Wilkinsons.

CHAPTER 12

Margot heard the footsteps behind her just as the door opened and Lela stood on the other side. Adam joined her the next instant and she was incredibly grateful that he'd seen her walking across the lodge and decided to join her. She needed him to hear what she had to ask the Wilkinsons.

"Margot, Adam, what can I do for you?"

"May we come in for a few minutes?" Margot asked, looking to Adam and then back to her. "I have a few questions that I think you can help me answer."

"I suppose so." She nodded and turned to look at Stan where he stood by the large fireplace, his arm propped up with a cup of coffee in one hand.

"What is it you want to know?"

"Tell me about your son," she said.

It was no surprise to her that both Lela and Stan's gazes snapped to hers. "Our…son?"

"Yes, I think he is involved in all of this somehow."

"No." Stan shook his head. "He couldn't be. He-he couldn't."

"Why do you say that?" Margot asked, catching Adam's sideways glance at her. She had a feeling he was probably wondering why she hadn't told him about this new development before now.

"B-because, he's banned from the resort." Lela's shoulders slumped, as any mother's would when talking about a wayward son.

"He's not allowed back on the grounds and he knows it. We made it very clear."

Margot nodded. "I know, but I have a feeling he *is* back and somehow involved in what's going on with CeCe."

"Why would you say that?" Lela's hands trembled as they dropped to her lap.

"I heard a rumor, and I'll say I realize it was *just* that, that you have grown very fond of CeCe."

"You know that already," Stan said, his tone indignant.

"Yes, but I needed your confirmation of that. You see, I've been thinking about the reason behind all of these attacks on CeCe. I keep wondering why she is the target of this when there seems to be *no* reason."

"Her ex-husband Rick has to be behind all of this. I know that's what CeCe was saying," Lela said.

"Unfortunately," Adam broke in, "he's no longer a possibility."

"He isn't?" Stan looked concerned.

"No."

"Which is what drew me back to this question again. *Why* CeCe? There is no reason for it. That is, until I heard the rumor that you two may be considering adding her into your will."

Lela gasped, covering her mouth with her hand. "Y-you think that Chris is behind all of this because of that?"

"I do. It's the only logical explanation. Who has the most to gain by CeCe being scared away from the resort?"

"Chris," Stan said, his voice barely above a whisper.

"Exactly."

"Our appointment…" Lela looked at Stan. "Should we cancel it?"

"What appointment?" Adam asked.

"We've finally scheduled an appointment with our lawyer to have the will changed. It took a lot of heart searching to decide if it really was what we wanted to do. We love CeCe, but Chris *is* our son. We finally decided to do it, though."

Stan pulled over a laptop and pressed a few buttons. From Margot's vantage point, she saw a program that looked a lot like the room entrance log. After tapping a few buttons, he nodded definitively.

"Yes, it's confirmed, our meeting is this afternoon at three. Doc Benson is coming up to meet with us."

"Doc Benson?" Adam asked.

"He's the doctor and a lawyer. He's handled all of our legal dealings from when we first started the resort until now."

"Have you told anyone about this?"

"No." Stan shook his head. "We don't often share our personal business. We just knew that CeCe would be the best option to pass down our legacy to. We only had Chris and when things went wrong with him…we thought we'd have to let the resort go. It would have been devastating to see our legacy disappear, but…"

"Have you had contact with Chris recently?" Adam easily slipped into his detective mode.

"No, not recently. We heard from him about a year ago. Had a big blow up—which was typical of our interactions —and I told him, again, that he was not welcome back at the resort. That was the last time we'd seen him."

"How well does he know this area?" Margot asked, thinking of the trail behind CeCe's cabin.

"He grew up here. He knows this area like the back of his

hand." Lela wiped a tear from the corner of her eye. "You've got to understand, we love our son but there was no way we could allow him near us or this resort. He'd stolen money from the safe, took one of our resort cars and crashed it, and even terrorized some of our guests. This was years ago, of course, but still we hadn't seen significant change in him when we met him a year ago so we knew we had to hold to our original decision of keeping him banned from the resort."

"No, I understand, it sounds like it was a difficult decision yet one you needed to make."

"Margot," Stan said, leaning forward with his elbows on his knees, "What do you think is going on here?"

Margot looked toward Adam and then back to the Wilkinsons. "I'm not sure, but I have a feeling Chris somehow found out about CeCe and your decision to make her your new beneficiary. I think he's doing what he can to drive her from the resort."

"Doesn't that seem a little extreme?" Lela said.

"It is unorthodox," Margot agreed.

"And yet, not unheard of. People come up with all sorts of plans that don't seem to make sense. It may not be logical, but I have a feeling he has a plan—if he is the one behind this."

"And if he's not?"

"Then there is someone else behind this."

"Oh my goodness," Lela said, covering her mouth. "Do you think Chris is behind Darren's death?"

Margot swallowed. "I'm not sure."

The Wilkinsons leaned back, looking at one another. Stan reached out and grasped Lela's hand, nodding at her. "Well, is there anything you can do? Should we bring Detective Rexton into this?"

"I don't know that we have enough information for him to make an arrest at this point. Not to mention the fact we don't know where Chris is," Adam said, "but I'll have a conversation with him. Just to bring him into the loop so that, should we come across Chris, there is less to explain about the situation that's playing out right now."

"If you think that's best," Stan said with resignation.

"I do." Adam stood up and Margot followed him.

"I'm sorry," Margot said, looking between the couple. "I know it's not easy for you. We will get to the bottom of this, though."

The Wilkinsons nodded and Margot and Adam left, the somber tone following them.

"Why didn't you tell me about this before?" Adam asked.

"I'm sorry." Margot had been expecting this question. "I only just put it together myself. I talked with Alice and she mentioned Chris—the first time I'd heard of him. I understand why the Wilkinsons wouldn't want to advertise their estranged son, but I had a feeling they'd considered him in part of this. Or maybe that I was just observing something I *thought* was there. Either way, I'm glad that it's out in the open."

"So you really think he's behind this?"

They walked out of the lodge and stopped. "I don't know. It just logically makes sense. He actually has a motive."

"Do you think he was involved with Darren Stevens' death then?"

It was a question Margot had been asking herself since she'd learned of Chris's existence. "I think it's too much of a coincidence."

"Then why hasn't he just killed CeCe?" Adam asked, leaning in so they wouldn't be overheard.

"I'm really not sure." Then Margot remembered Jenny entering CeCe's cabin. "Oh! We need to get to CeCe's cabin before she does."

"Why?"

As they made their way down the path to their cabins, Margot explained what she'd seen.

"Why didn't you tell me before? We could have caught her in the act."

"Yes," Margot agreed, "but with this new information, I'm even more convinced that I think she is working in tandem with Chris. To apprehend her before the right time could send Chris into hiding and we'd never find him. We can find Jenny after this and talk with her, maybe we can convince her to give up Chris." They reached CeCe's cabin and Margot pulled out the extra key CeCe had given her. "At least this way we can discover what—if anything—Jenny planted in her cabin before CeCe sees it. Maybe save her some trauma."

Adam nodded and insisted he go in before Margot just in case. He pushed the door open and Margot took a step in, but ran into his back.

"*Oomph.*" She stepped back. "What is it? What's wrong?"

"I think our plans have changed."

"What do you mean?" Margot asked, trying to peer around Adam.

"I just found Jenny."

Adam shifted and Margot finally got a look around his shoulder to see Jenny sprawled on the floor. She was dead.

"This Jenny character is *not* who she said she was." Detective Rexton shook his head, pacing in the corner of the dining area he'd taken over as his command area. Dealing with two murders now, the vein in his head was standing out more vibrantly than Margot had ever seen it. Miraculously, after Adam had explained to him who he was and shown his credentials, the surly detective had begun to treat them both with more respect.

Margot also wondered if desperation had anything to do with it. It had been several days since Darren's body had been discovered and they still had no solid leads.

"What do you mean?" she asked, looking from Rexton to Adam and then back again.

"We ran a background check on her. She's got prior arrests like you wouldn't believe."

"What about Ron?" Margot asked.

"Questioned him." Rexton shook his head. "He's a dead end—pardon the phrase. Turns out that Ron Durk is an actor. He was hired by Jenny Blane to accompany her to this resort. He wasn't very clear on the details, but he did know that Jenny wasn't happy when he showed up. Mentioned something about the fact that his headshot was dated and he was much older than what she'd been looking for."

"She wanted someone closer to her age. Maybe to play the role of boyfriend better?" Margot asked.

"That's what I think. It was clear that she wasn't here for the resort itself, but Ron couldn't give us helpful information about why she *was* here. He said that she was gone most of the day and only did a few things with him."

"So she's working with Chris," Margot said, almost to herself.

"Now that I know all of what's going on," Rexton said, his gaze displaying his displeasure, "I'd say that is accurate. She was apparently in CeCe's cabin for a reason—we found the cleaning supplies so she was obviously the one cleaning it—but it looked like someone could have lured her there to kill her."

"Maybe she's outlasted her usefulness," Margot mused.

"You think Chris is cleaning up?"

"I think he's realizing that his games aren't working," Adam said, "and he's stepped up his efforts."

"So you think that CeCe's in danger then?" Rexton said, looking between Adam and Margot.

"I think she's been in danger this whole time," Margot said, taking a deep breath, "but now more than before."

"I'm sorry," Alice said, coming up behind them with a tray holding cups of steaming coffee. "I didn't mean to eavesdrop but I couldn't help hearing you mention Chris."

Margot smiled kindly at the young woman. "I promise I didn't out you to the Wilkinsons."

"Oh, I'm not worried. I understand. I mean…after all that's happened." The tray shook in her hands and Adam stepped forward to take it from her, setting it on a side table.

"I know it's upsetting," Margot said kindly, "but we're getting to the bottom of this."

"That's good." She nodded, a shaky hand pushing back a strand of her hair. "I just… It's all so crazy. You really think Chris is behind these terrible things?"

"We're not sure, miss," Detective Rexton said. "But any information you can tell me about this young man would be very helpful."

"I mean, there's not much to tell. I've known Chris since I was a young girl. He's just a few years older than me. He never was very nice so I didn't spend much time around him, but he is really smart. I know that for sure."

"What do you mean by that?" Adam asked.

"I don't know, he'd always be messing around with computers and things like that. He made dumb choices and got into lots of trouble, but when he wasn't partying, he actually did some pretty amazing things."

"Like what?" Margot prompted.

"Well, he created the whole computer system for the resort. The scheduling system, the cabin authorization logs, and even an app that employees can use for recording their duties and things like that. It's the same one they've used for years."

Margot sat up straighter. "He created the system?"

"Yeah…" Alice looked between Margot and the detectives. "Why?"

"Oh no. What time is it?"

137

"Uh, quarter to three," Rexton said, his frown deepening. "Why? What's going on?"

"We need to go. We need to get to the Wilkinsons. I have a feeling that the meeting with their lawyer isn't going to happen as scheduled."

CHAPTER 13

IN A RUSH OF MOVEMENT, MARGOT, ADAM, AND DETECTIVE Rexton rushed out of the dining hall and through the lodge. Startled, people turned to watch them, some of the officers stopping what they were doing to follow their leader to the back of the lodge and up the steps to the Wilkinsons' apartment.

"Is there another way up to this apartment?" Rexton asked in a hushed tone.

"No," Alice said. She'd been caught up in the rush to get to the apartment, something Margot was thankful for now.

"But there are cameras," she said.

This halted Rexton five steps from the top. "We need to cut that feed."

"We don't have time," Margot pleaded. "I saw the Wilkinsons' schedule when Stan checked it for their appointment. It was set for three and I have a feeling that Chris won't let them go through with changing the will."

"I'm inclined to agree with you," Adam said. "Here, let me go first."

Rexton stepped aside and Adam and Margot rushed up the steps. Adam knocked. "Stan, Lela? We've got an urgent situation that needs your attention."

"We're—busy," came a strained reply.

Margot looked to Adam and then shook her head. This wasn't good.

"It'll only take a second."

Adam tried the door and found that it was unlocked, something Margot was extremely grateful for, and they stepped into the darkened apartment.

Margot took in the scene before them. A dark-haired man stood in the middle of the living space, a gun pointed at Stan while Lela huddled next to him.

"You must be Chris," Margot said.

The man's eyes narrowed and his gaze flickered between Adam and Margot. "Who are you? How do you know who I am?"

"My name is Margot and this is my friend Adam."

"Margot. You're CeCe's friend."

"I am," she said, taking a step toward him.

"Stop. Don't come any closer."

"Hold on now," she said in a calming tone. "There's no need to make hasty decisions. I hear that you are good with computers."

He frowned, his gaze shifting again to the side then back to Margot.

"Yeah. So what?"

"So, let me tell you what I think is happening here." She paused but not to let him speak, only to take a slight step to the side and effectively make Chris follow her movements. "I think you found out about your parents' new chef, their pride and joy, and you started to sense that your inheritance was in danger. Surely you knew that there were problems—your parents had banned you from the resort—but perhaps you still thought they would allow you to inherit. Let the past go, perhaps. Or maybe forget they even had a will that you were named in. Either way, you finally started to see that your standing with them was threatened."

He didn't speak, but she took another step to the side.

"I think you saw CeCe as an opportunity. Get her away from your parents so they would be less likely to change their will. I also think you made a connection with Jenny. Somehow, maybe in the time between when you used to live here and when you decided to come back, you convinced her to join with you." Margot paced to the side even more, noticing the way Chris turned his head to watch her. "Maybe you even promised her part of your inheritance, but either way, you got her to clean CeCe's cabin and plant things there that were supposedly from her ex-husband Rick."

"You don't know what you're talking about."

"Don't I, Chris?" she asked, looking him in the eyes and stepping to the side again. "You couldn't let a stranger have what was rightfully yours. You couldn't stand to see your parents embrace someone else when they banned you from the resort."

"So? It wasn't right," Chris said, the gun slipping down a few inches. "I am their *son*, and what? She's just some woman they hired. How was I supposed to sit by and let them give what was rightfully mine to someone else?"

"Oh, Chris," Lela said, her voice wobbling.

"Quiet, Mom." He clenched his jaw. "I had a good plan. Jenny bought it too, thought I'd give her half of everything. She had no idea."

"So you found out about CeCe's past," Margot prompted.

"Yeah, I was friends with her ex-husband. He used to brag about how he followed her around, leaving her little notes and gifts. He knew it freaked her out so I thought I'd use his confession to my advantage. Seemed like a good idea to use that as a way to get her to leave. I mean, she holed up after he'd started harassing her the first time, it made sense she'd do it again."

"But she didn't," Margot said.

"No. I tried everything, but she wouldn't leave. I had to do something."

"So, you killed Rick." Margot said it bluntly, hoping to startle him, and it worked. A crazed look entered his eyes.

"I did. It was the only way. He had to die."

The next second, at the same time Chris dropped the gun a few more inches, Adam lunged out of the corner he'd slowly moved into. He collided with Chris, tackling him around the middle and taking him flying back over the antique white couch. They crashed onto the other side of the floor in a tangle of limbs.

Margot rushed to Stan and Lela, pulling them out of the way at the same moment that Detective Rexton and his officers came barging through the door. Two armed officers immediately rushed to where Adam had Chris pinned down.

"Chris Wilkinson," Detective Rexton said, "you are under arrest."

"HOW ABOUT SECONDS?" CeCe asked, standing in front of the table where Margot, Adam, and Detective Rexton sat in the back of the dining room the next morning.

"I couldn't even *think* about seconds without needing to run five miles," Adam said, hand on his trim waist.

"How about you, Sal?" she said, a sly grin on her face.

"As much as I *wish* I could eat more, there's no way I'd find anywhere to put it all." He smiled, shocking both Margot and CeCe, who shared a look over the detective's head when he turned to look at Adam. "But it was mighty fine."

Once they had apprehended Chris, Detective Rexton had suddenly become a different person. It was as if the stress had brought out the worst in him, but with the resolution of the difficult case, he'd relaxed some. Margot had to admit she liked this version of the detective much better.

"I'm glad you liked it," CeCe said, beaming.

Margot let out a deep, satisfied breath watching her friend finally begin to relax. It had only been a day, and yet that had already made a big difference.

"You'll all be happy to note that Chris is under lock and key and the case against him is strong."

"I don't know if I'd say happy," Margot said, watching as CeCe sat down to join them, "but I *am* glad. It's difficult to think of Stan and Lela having to deal with this, but I'm *so* glad that it's all come to a close."

Rexton nodded. "Very true."

"Can you tell me what happen?" CeCe asked.

Rexton looked as if he was about to say no, but then the

corner of his mouth came up in another uncharacteristic smile. It would seem as if CeCe had captured the detective's attention.

"Once he realized we had him on tape, thanks to the extreme sensitivity of the Wilkinson's' recording devices, he confessed pretty quickly."

"When I heard of Rick's death," Margot said, sending a glance toward CeCe, "I had a feeling we were dealing with someone who had undergone a psychotic break or something of the sort."

"Yes, you're right. He saw the need to take Rick's life as essential to his mission. Thankfully, he hadn't considered killing his parents—though I have no doubt he might have sought that as an option if all else had failed."

"But he was responsible for Darren *and* Jenny's death?" CeCe asked.

"Yes." Detective Rexton tossed his napkin on his plate, leaning back. "He said that he'd just come out of CeCe's cabin when Darren caught him. He acted quickly and sadly ended Darren's life, but again, he justified it with the thought that he was accomplishing his personal mission. He turned on Jenny because that had always been a part of the plan."

"But how did he get up here in the first place?" CeCe asked.

"It turns out that—"

"There's a cabin, further in the woods. Isn't there?" Margot asked.

"Yes. How did you know?"

"The same way I *knew* he had put that snake in my cabin. I was on the trail ride with Bubb and he'd told me a little bit about the area. Said there was a cabin off in the woods, but only people who really knew the area would know where it was. I had no way to prove it, but I had a feeling that he could have been staying there. I suppose if you look at the back of the clearing behind CeCe's cabin, you'll find a small trail that will lead to it."

"And what about the snake?" Adam asked, looking intently at Margot because he knew she hated snakes.

"On that same ride, Jenny's horse had reared up due to a snake in the path. I was beginning to suspect there was more to Jenny at that time because she'd told me she didn't know how to ride, but she'd handled that horse like a pro. And then when she lied about being lactose intolerant to one of your officers, it again made me suspicious."

"Yes, she was connected with Chris because of a short term in prison that he did when he was younger. They'd stayed in touch—when she wasn't in jail—and therefore made a perfect accessory to his plan. Unfortunately, she didn't know his true intention."

"So sad," CeCe said, running her finger over the rim of her coffee cup.

"Well," Rexton said, standing up and pulling on his hat. "I just want to say that, despite what I first thought, you were a big help, Missus Durand."

Margot smirked. "Why thank you, Detective Rexton."

"Sal," he said. Then he turned his gaze toward CeCe. "Missus Baxter, it's been a pleasure. Thank you kindly for inviting me for breakfast. Despite the circumstances, it's been nice getting to know you."

"Same to you, Detective Rexton."

"It's Sal, remember?" he said with a grin and a wink.

"Then it's CeCe," she replied with an equally happy smile.

Margot's eyebrows rose as Sal leaned down. "Maybe I could take you to coffee sometime."

CeCe giggled like a schoolgirl, blushing thoroughly. "I'd like that."

He nodded then spun around and left the dining hall, whistling a happy tune.

"Well, that was unexpected," Margot said.

CeCe giggled again. "You can say that again."

"I'm not sure what just happened," Adam added, looking between the two.

"Looks like Sal conquered his distrust of CeCe and I to come out the other side with a friend."

Adam shook his head, but CeCe leaned over toward Margot. "I can't thank you enough."

"I had nothing to do with the detective's advances," Margot said with a grin.

"Oh, you know what I mean. For helping me with figuring out this whole thing. I...I can't believe what happened, but I *am* thankful that you were here to help me."

"Greed is a funny thing. It affects so many," Adam observed.

"Do you really think it was only greed, though? I think that, somewhere in Chris's mind, he saw CeCe as taking over his rightful spot here at the resort. He went about it completely the wrong way, but I think he just wanted to make things right with his family."

"That seems a little naive, doesn't it?" Adam asked.

"Not completely. Either way, he was wrong and will serve the punishment for his crimes."

"Margot, I'm sorry for ruining your vacation."

Margot laughed, thinking of how she was destined to experience vacations that involved mysteries. "I would rather help out a friend in need than anything else. Thank you for finding a way for us to stay an extra day."

"It was no problem. Stan and Lela wanted you to stay for another week, but I knew you'd want to get back to your bakery. But I figured I could convince you to stay for one extra day."

"You're right," Margot said, laughing. "I convinced myself that the shop would be all right for one more day without me, but I don't think I could stay away for much more."

They chuckled at this, both knowing how much she loved her shop and hated to be away from it for too long.

They chatted for a little while longer then rose to say good-bye. Margot hugged her friend tightly, asking her to stay in touch, and especially to let her know how the coffee date went with Detective Rexton. Assured that she would, Margot and Adam walked out of the lodge into the splendor of the Blue Ridge Mountains.

"Do you feel like you've missed seeing the beauty around you since you've been so focused on helping CeCe?"

"Yes and no," she said, taking him by the hand and pulling him gently toward the small path that led up to the vista point she'd come to on her first day at the resort. "Yes, in that I would have liked to spend more time here with you." She looked around at the beauty and took a deep breath. "But no, in the sense that I'm glad I could help CeCe. I hated to see her so afraid, and the Wilkinsons too. I'm glad they've found each other."

"Me too. It sounds like CeCe is the right choice to take over the resort. Who knows? Maybe she'll want a pastry chef on staff."

"And leave my bakery? Adam Eastwood, you know me better than that."

The rich sound of his deep laugh made her smile even more as he slipped his arm around her shoulders. They took in the view in silence and Margot thought again of her shop. She missed the community of North Bank. Her regulars like Bentley and the other residents from the neighboring senior living communities, as well as her part-time helper Rosie.

"No," she said, resting her head against Adam's shoulder, "I think it's time to go home."

$\sim$

THANK YOU!

Thanks for reading *Vacations and Violence*. I hope you enjoyed reading the story as much as I enjoyed writing it. If you did, it would be awesome if you left a review for me on Amazon and/or Goodreads.

If you would like to know about future cozy mysteries by me and the other authors at Fairfield Publishing, make sure to sign up for our Cozy Mystery Newsletter. We will send you our FREE Cozy Mystery Starter Library just for signing up. All the details are on the next page.

At the very end of the book, I have included a couple previews of books by friends and fellow authors at

Fairfield Publishing. First is a preview of *Up in Smoke* by Shannon VanBergen - it's the first book in the Glock Grannies Cozy Mystery series. Second is a preview of *A Pie to Die For* by Stacey Alabaster - it's part of the popular Bakery Detectives Cozy Mystery series. I really hope you like the samples. If you do, both books are available on Amazon.

- Get Up in Smoke here:
  amazon.com/dp/B06XHKYRRX

- Get A Pie to Die For here:
  amazon.com/dp/B01D6ZVT78

FAIRFIELD COZY MYSTERY NEWSLETTER

Make sure you sign up for the Fairfield Cozy Mystery Newsletter so you can keep up with our latest releases. When you sign up, **we will send you our FREE Cozy Mystery Starter Library!**

FairfieldPublishing.com/cozy-newsletter/

After you sign up to get your Free Starter Library, turn the page and check out the free previews :)

I COULD FEEL MY HAIR PUFFING UP LIKE COTTON CANDY IN the humidity as I stepped outside the Miami airport. I pushed a sticky strand from my face, and I wished for a minute that it were a cheerful pink instead of dirty blond, just to complete the illusion.

"Thank you so much for picking me up from the airport." I smiled at the sprightly old lady I was struggling to keep up with. "But why did you say my grandmother couldn't pick me up?"

"I didn't say." She turned and gave me a toothy grin—clearly none of them original—and winked. "I parked over here."

When we got to her car, she opened the trunk and threw in the sign she had been holding when she met me in baggage claim. The letters were done in gold glitter glue and she had drawn flowers with markers all around the edges. My name "Nikki Rae Parker" flashed when the sun reflected off of them, temporarily blinding me.

"I can tell you put a lot of work into that sign." I carefully put my luggage to the side of it, making sure not to touch her sign—partially because I didn't want to crush it and partially because it didn't look like the glue had dried yet.

"Well, your grandmother didn't give me much time to make it. I only had about ten minutes." She glanced at the sign proudly before closing the trunk. She looked me in the eyes. "Let's get on the road. We can chit chat in the car."

With that, she climbed in and clicked on her seat belt. As I got in, she was applying a thick coat of bright red lipstick while looking in the rearview mirror. "Gotta look sharp in case we get pulled over." She winked again, her heavily wrinkled eyelid looking like it thought about staying closed before it sprung back up again.

I thought about her words for a moment. She must get

pulled over a lot, I thought. Poor old lady. I could picture her going ten miles an hour while the rest of Miami flew by her.

"Better buckle up." She pinched her lips together before blotting them slightly on a tissue. She smiled at me and for a moment, I was jealous of her pouty lips, every line filled in by layers and layers of red.

I did as I was told and buckled my seat belt before I sunk down into her caramel leather seats. I was exhausted, both physically and mentally, from the trip. I closed my eyes and tried to forget my troubles, taking in a deep breath and letting it out slowly to give all my worry and fear ample time to escape my body. For the first time since I had made the decision to come here, I felt at peace. Unfortunately, it was short-lived.

The sound of squealing tires filled the air and my eyes flung open to see this old lady zigzagging through the parking garage. She took the turns without hitting the brakes, hugging each curve like a racecar driver. When we exited the garage and turned onto the street, she broke out in laughter. "That's my favorite part!"

I tugged my seat belt to make sure it was on tight. This was not going to be the relaxing drive I had thought it would be.

We hit the highway and I felt like I was in an arcade game. She wove in and out of traffic at a speed I was sure matched her old age.

"Ya know, the older I get the worse other people drive." She took one hand off the wheel and started to rummage through her purse, which sat between us.

"Um, can I help you with something?" My nerves were starting to get the best of me as her eyes were focused more on her purse than the road.

"Oh no, I've got it. I'm sure it's in here somewhere." She dug a little more, pulling out a package of AA batteries and then a ham sandwich.

Brake lights lit up in front of us and I screamed, bracing myself for impact. The old woman glanced up and pulled the car to the left in a quick jerk before returning to her purse. Horns blared from behind us.

"There it is!" She pulled out a package of wintergreen Life Savers. "Do you want one?"

"No, thank you." I could barely get the words out.

"I learned a long time ago that it was easier if I just drove and did my thing instead of worrying about what all the other drivers were doing. It's easier for them to get out of my way instead of me getting out of theirs. My reflexes aren't what they used to be." She popped a mint in her mouth and smiled. "I love wintergreen. I don't know why peppermint is more popular. Peppermint is so stuffy; wintergreen is fun."

She seemed to get in a groove with her driving and soon my grip was loosening on the sides of the seat, the blood slowly returning to my knuckles. Suddenly I realized I hadn't asked her name.

"I was so confused when you picked me up from the airport instead of my Grandma Dean that I never asked your name."

She didn't respond, just kept her eyes on the road with a steely look on her face. I was happy to see her finally being serious about driving, so I turned to look out the window. "It's beautiful here," I said after a few minutes of silence. I turned to look at her again and noticed that she was still focused straight ahead. I stared at her for a moment and realized she never blinked. Panic rose through my chest.

"Ma'am!" I shouted as I leaned forward to take the wheel. "Are you okay?"

She suddenly sprung to action, screaming and jerking the wheel to the left. Her screaming caused me to scream and I grabbed the wheel and pulled it to the right, trying to get us back in our lane. We continued to scream until the car stopped teetering and settled down to a nice hum on the road.

"Are you trying to kill us?" The woman's voice was hoarse and she seemed out of breath.

"I tried to talk to you and you didn't answer!" I practically shouted. "I thought you had a heart attack or something!"

"You almost gave me one!" She flashed me a dirty look.

"And you made me swallow my mint. You're lucky I didn't choke to death!"

"I'm sorry." As I said the words, I noticed my heart was beating in my ears. "I really thought something had happened to you."

She was quiet for a moment. "Well, to be honest with you, I did doze off for a moment." She looked at me, pride spreading across her face. "I sleep with my eyes open. Do you know anyone who can do that?"

Before I could answer, she was telling me about her friend Delores who "claimed" she could sleep with her eyes open but, as it turned out, just slept with one eye half-open because she had a stroke and it wouldn't close all the way.

I sat there in silence before saying a quick prayer. My hands resumed their spot around the seat cushion and I could feel the blood draining from my knuckles yet again.

"So what was it you tried to talk to me about before you nearly killed us?"

I swallowed hard, trying to push away the irritation that fought to come out.

"I asked you what your name was." I stared at her and decided right then that I wouldn't take my eyes off of her for the rest of the trip. I would make sure she stayed awake, even if it meant talking to her the entire time.

"Oh yes! My name is Hattie Sue Miller," she said with a bit of arrogance. She glanced at me. "My father used to own most of this land." She motioned to either side of us. "Until he sold it and made a fortune." She gave me a look and dropped her voice to a whisper as she raised one eyebrow. "Of course we don't talk about money. That would be inappropriate." She said that last part like I had just asked her when she had last had sex. I felt ashamed until I realized I had never asked her about her money; I had simply asked her name. This woman was a nut. Didn't Grandma Dean have any other friends she could've sent to get me?

For the next hour or so, I asked her all kinds of questions to keep her awake—none of them about money or anything I thought might lead to money. If what she told me was true, she had a very interesting upbringing. She claimed to be related to Julia Tuttle, the woman who founded Miami. Her stories of how she got a railroad company to agree to build tracks there were fascinating. It wasn't until she told me she was also related to Michael Jackson that I started to question how true her stories were.

"We're almost there! Geraldine will be so happy to see you. You're all she's talked about the last two weeks." She pulled into a street lined with palm trees. "You're going to love it here." She smiled as she drove. "I've lived here a long time. It's far enough away from the city that you don't have all that hullaballoo, but big enough that you can eat at a different restaurant every day for a month."

When we entered the downtown area, heavy gray smoke

hung in the air, and the road was blocked by a fire truck and two police cars.

"Oh no! I think there might have been a fire!" I leaned forward in my seat, trying to get a better look.

"Of course there was a fire!" Hattie huffed like I was an idiot. "That's why Geraldine sent me to get you!"

"What?! Is she okay?" I scanned the crowd and saw her immediately. She was easy to spot, even at our distance.

"Oh yes. She's fine. Her shop went up in flames as she was headed out the door. She got the call from a neighboring store owner and called me right away to go get you. Honestly, I barely had time to make you a sign." She acted like Grandma Dean had really put her in a bad position, leaving her only minutes to get my name on a piece of poster board.

Hattie pulled over and I jumped out; I'd come back for my luggage later. As I made my way toward the crowd, I was amazed at how little my Grandma Dean—or Grandma Dean-Dean, as I had called her since I was a little girl— had changed. Her bleach blonde hair was nearly white and cut in a cute bob that was level with her chin. She wore skintight light blue denim capris, which hugged her tiny frame. Her bright white t-shirt was the background for a long colorful necklace that appeared to be a string of beads. Thanks to a pair of bright red heels, she stood eye to eye with the fireman she was talking to.

I ran up to her and called out to her. "Grandma! Are you

okay?" She flashed me a look of disgust before she smiled weakly at the fireman and said something I couldn't make out.

She turned her back to him and grabbed me by the arm. "I told you to never call me that!" She softened her tone then looked me over. "You look exhausted! Was it the flight or riding with that crazy Hattie?" She didn't give me time to answer. "Joe, this is my daughter's daughter, Nikki."

Joe smiled. I wasn't sure if it was his perfectly white teeth that got my attention, his uniform or his sparkling blue eyes, but I was immediately speechless. I tried to say hello, but the words stuck in my throat.

"Nikki, this is Joe Dellucci. He was born in New Jersey but his parents came from Italy. Isn't that right, Joe?"

I was disappointed when Joe answered without a New Jersey accent. Grandma Dean continued to tell me about Joe's heritage, which reminded me of Hattie. Apparently once you got to a certain age, you automatically became interested in people's backgrounds.

He must have noticed the look of disappointment on my face. "My family moved here when I was ten. My accent only slips in when I'm tired." His face lit up with a smile, causing mine to do the same. "Or when I eat pizza." I had no idea what he meant by that, but it caused me to break out in nervous laughter. Grandma Dean's look of embarrassment finally snapped me out of it.

"Well, Miss Dean. If I hear anything else, I'll let you know.

In the meantime, call your insurance company. I'm sure they'll get you in touch with a good fire restoration service. If not, let me know. My brother's in the business."

He handed her a business card and I saw the name in red letters across the front: *Clean-up Guys*. Not a very catchy name. Then suddenly it hit me. A fireman with a brother who does fire restoration? Seemed a little fishy. Joe must have noticed my expression, because he chimed in. "Our house burned down when I was eight and Alex was twelve. I guess it had an impact on us."

Grandma Dean took the card and put it in her back pocket. "Thanks, Joe. I'll give Alex a call this afternoon."

They said their good-byes and as Joe walked away, Grandma Dean turned toward me. "What did I tell you about calling me 'Grandma' in public?" Her voice was barely over a whisper. "I've given you a list of names that are appropriate and I don't understand why you don't use one of them!"

"I'm not calling you Coco!" My mind tried to think of the other names on the list. Peaches? Was that on there? Whatever it was, they all sounded ridiculous.

"There is nothing wrong with Coco!" She pulled away from me and ran a hand through her hair as a woman approached us.

"Geraldine, I'm so sorry to hear about the fire!" The woman hugged Grandma Dean. "Do they know what started it?"

"No, but Joe's on it. He'll figure it out. I'm sure it was wiring or something. You know how these old buildings are."

The woman nodded in agreement. "If you need anything, please let me know." She hugged Grandma again and gave her a look of pity.

"Bev, this is my...daughter's daughter, Nikki."

I rolled my eyes. She couldn't even say granddaughter. I wondered if she would come up with some crazy name to replace that too.

"It's nice to meet you," Bev said without actually looking at me. She looked worried. Her drawn-on eyebrows were pinched together, creating a little bulge between them. "If you hear anything about what started it, please be sure to let me know."

Grandma turned to me as the woman walked away. "She owns the only other antique store on this block. I'm sure she's happy as a clam that her competition is out for a while," Grandma said, almost with a laugh.

I gasped. "Do you think she did it? Do you think she set fire to your shop?"

"Oh, honey, don't go jumping to conclusions like that. She would never hurt a fly." Grandma looked around. "Where's your luggage?"

I turned to point toward Hattie's car, but it was gone.

165

Grandma let out a loud laugh. "Hattie took off with your luggage? Well, then let's go get it."

THANKS FOR READING the sample of *Up in Smoke*. I really hope you liked it. You can read the rest at:

- **amazon.com/dp/B06XHKYRRX**

MAKE sure you turn to the next page for the preview of *A Pie to Die For*.

PREVIEW: A PIE TO DIE FOR

"But you don't understand, I use only the finest, organic ingredients." My voice was high-pitched as I pleaded my case to the policeman. Oh, this was just like an episode of Criminal Point. Hey, I wondered who the killer turned out to be. I shook my head. That's not important, Rachael, I scolded myself. *What's important is getting yourself off this murder charge.* Still, I hoped Pippa had recorded the ending of the episode.

I tried to steady my breathing as Jackson—Detective Whitaker—entered the room and threw a folder on the table, before studying the contents as though he was cramming for a test he had to take the next day. He rubbed his temples and frowned.

Is he even going to make eye contact with me? Is he just going to completely ignore the interaction we had at the fair? Pretend it never even happened.

"Jackson..." I started, before I was met with a steely glare. "Detective. Surely you can't think I had anything to do with this?"

Jackson looked up at me slowly. "Had you ever had any contact with Mrs. Batters before today?"

I shifted in my seat. "Yes," I had to admit. "I knew her a little from the store. She was always quite antagonistic towards me, but I'd never try to kill her!"

"Witnesses near the scene said that you two had an argument." He gave me that same steely glare. Where was the charming, flirty, sweet guy I'd meet earlier? He was now buried beneath a suit and a huge attitude.

"Well...it wasn't an argument...she was just...winding me up, like she always does."

Jackson shot me a sharp look. "So, she was annoying you? Was she making you angry?"

"Well... Well..." I tripped over my words. He was now making me nervous for an entirely different reason than he had earlier. Those butterflies were back, but now they felt like daggers.

Come on, Rach. Everyone knows that the first suspect in Criminal Point is not the one that actually did it.

But how many people had Jackson already interviewed? Maybe he was saving me for last. Gosh, maybe my cherry pie had actually killed the woman!

"Answer the question please, Miss Robinson."

"Not angry, no. I was just frustrated."

"Frustrated?" A smile curled at his lips before he pounced. "Frustrated with Mrs. Batters?"

"No! The situation. Come on—you were there!" I tried to appeal to his sympathies, but he remained a brick wall.

"It doesn't matter whether I was there or not. That is entirely besides the point." He said the words a little too forcefully.

I swallowed. "I couldn't get any customers to try my cakes, and Bakermatic was luring everyone away with their free samples." I stopped as my brows shot up involuntarily. "Jackson! Sorry, Detective. Mrs. Batters ate at Bakermatic as well!"

My words came out in a stream of breathless blabber as I raced to get them out. "Bakermatic must be to blame! They cut corners, they use cheap ingredients. Oh, and I know how much Mrs. Batters loved their food! She was always eating there. Believe me, she made that very clear to me."

Jackson sat back and folded his arms across his chest. "Don't try to solve this case for us."

I sealed my lips. *Looks like I might have to at this rate.*

"We are investigating every place Mrs. Batters ate today. You don't need to worry about that."

I leaned forward and banged my palm on the table. "But I do need to worry about it! This is my job, my livelihood... my life on the line. If people think I am to blame, that will be the final nail in my bakery's coffin!" Oh, what a day. And I'd thought it was bad enough that I hadn't gotten any customers at my stand. Now I was being accused of killing a woman!

I could have sworn I saw a flicker of sympathy finally crawl across Jackson's face. He stood up and readjusted his tie, but he still refused to make full eye contact. "You're free to go, Miss Robinson," he said gently. There was that tone from earlier, finally. He seemed recognizable as a human at long last.

"Really?"

He nodded. "For the moment. But we might have some more questions for you later, so don't leave town."

I tried to make eye contact with him as I left, squirreling out from underneath his arm as he held the door open for me, but he just kept staring at the floor.

Did that mean he wasn't coming back to my bakery after all?

~

PIPPA WAS STILL WAITING for me when I returned home later that evening. There was a chill in the air, which meant that I headed straight for a blanket and the fireplace when I finally crawled in through the door. Pippa shot me a sympathetic look as I curled up and crumbled in front of the flames. *How had today gone so wrong, so quickly?*

"I recorded the last part of the show," Pippa said softly. "If you're up for watching it."

I groaned and lay on the carpet, my back straight against the floor like I was a little kid. "I don't think I can stomach it after what I just went through. Can you believe it? Accusing ME of killing Mrs. Batters? When I *know* that Bakermatic is to blame. I mean, Pippa, they must be! But this detective wouldn't even listen to me when I was trying to explain Bakermatic's dodgy practices to him."

Pippa leaned forward and took the lid off a pot, the smell of the brew hitting my nose. "Pippa, what is that?"

She grinned and stirred it, which only made the smell worse. I leaned back and covered my nose. "Thought it might be a bit heavy for you. I basically took every herb, tea, and spice that you had in your cabinet and came up with this! I call it 'Pippa's Delight'!"

"Yeah well, it doesn't sound too delightful." I sat up and scrunched up my nose. "Oh, what the heck—pour me a cup."

"Are you sure?" Pippa asked with a cheeky grin.

"Go on. I'll be brave."

I braced myself as the brown liquid hit the white mug.

It was as disgusting as I had imagined, but at least it made me laugh when the pungent concoction hit my tongue. Pippa always had a way of cheering me up. If it wasn't her unusual concoctions, or her ever changing hair color— red this week but pink the last, and purple a week before that—then it was her never-ending array of careers and job changes that entertained me and kept me on my toes. When you're trying to run your own business, forced to be responsible day in and day out, you have to live vicariously through some of your more free-spirited friends. And Pippa was definitely that: free-spirited.

"Hey!" I said suddenly, as an idea began to brew in my brain. I didn't know if it was the tea that suddenly brought all my senses to life or what it was, but I found myself slamming my mug on the table with new found enthusiasm. "Pippa, have you got a job at the moment?" I could never keep up with Pippa's present state of employment.

She shrugged as she kicked her feet up and lay back on the sofa. "Not really! I mean, I've got a couple of things in the works. Why's that?"

I pondered for a moment. "Pippa, if you could get a job at Bakermatic, you could see first hand what they're up to!" My voice was a rush of excitement as I clapped my hands together. "You would get to find out the ways they cut corners, the bad ingredients they use, and, if you were really lucky, you might even overhear someone say something about Mrs. Batters!"

A gleam appeared in Pippa's green eyes. "Well, I do need a job, especially after today."

I raced on. "Yes! And you've got plenty of experience working in cafes."

"Yeah. I've worked in hundreds of places." She took a sip of the tea and managed to swallow it. She actually seemed to enjoy it.

"I know you've got a lot of experience. You're sure to get the job. They're always looking for part-timers." Unfortunately, Bakermatic was planning on expanding the storefront even further, and that meant they were looking for even more employees to fill their big yellow store. "Pippa, this is the perfect plan! We'll get you an application first thing in the morning. Then you can start investigating!"

Pippa raised her eyebrows. "Investigating?"

I nodded and lay my head back down on the carpet. "Criminal Point—Belldale Style! Bakery Investigation Unit! I will investigate and do what I can from my end as well! Perhaps I could talk to people from all the other food stalls! Oh, Pippa, we're going to make a crack team of detectives!"

"The Bakery Detectives!"

We both started giggling but, as the full weight of the day's events started to pile up on me, I felt my stomach tighten. It might seem fun to send Pippa in to spy on

Bakermatic, but this was serious. My bakery, my livelihood, and even my own freedom depended on it.

THANKS FOR READING a sample of my book, *A Pie to Die For*. I really hope you liked it. You can read the rest at:

amazon.com/dp/B01D6ZVT78

OR YOU CAN GET it for free by signing up for our newsletter.

FairfieldPublishing.com/cozy-newsletter/

amazon.com/dp/B01D6ZVT78

Made in United States
North Haven, CT
13 November 2022

26657819R00107